MW00714013

# The Trouble With Tea

*To Gail —*
*Good reading!*

# The Trouble With Tea

*Jeanette E. Alsheimer*

Jeanette E. Alsheimer
Patricia J. Friedle

*Patricia J. Friedle*

Pentland Press, Inc.
www.pentlandpressusa.com

PUBLISHED BY PENTLAND PRESS, INC.
5122 Bur Oak Circle, Raleigh, North Carolina 27612
United States of America
919-782-0281

ISBN 1-57197-299-4
Library of Congress Control Number: 2001 132674

Printed in the United States of America

Dedicated to Trudy Van Wyck Leary and Mae Jones Fitzgerald
who enthusiastically supported, but never saw the end result.

Acknowledgments

We thank our husbands and children for their patience and good humor during our lengthy efforts. We gratefully acknowledge those, especially Greg, who so willingly read and reread.

## Boston 1770

The red-coated sentry found it hard to stand at attention with the frigid March wind stinging his face. Guard duty at the Boston Customs House was never a choice assignment, but then Captain Preston was clearly angry with him. Punishment is what it was. Maybe trying to steal a kiss with the pretty colonial was not the smartest thing he had ever done, but what else was there to relieve the boredom in this forsaken place. The family who had been forced to house him certainly did not want him. They'd made that clear enough.

To take his mind off his numbed feet, he started to count the pigeons huddled together on the rooftops. Afterwards he would look for Jim, that new soldier who seemed so friendly. Some dark ale and an ear to bend, that'd be the ticket.

The first snowball smashed hard into the back of his head, drawing blood. His sharp cry was almost drowned in the shower of more balls of ice. Men rushed toward him, their arms upraised. He turned to run, but his feet slid out from under him. Stunned by the impact of frozen ground, he prayed that God would not to let him die here so far from home.

He was conscious of loud voices and the fast approach of threatening footsteps. He heard Captain Preston's shouts to hurry. A blur of red coats appeared, fighting their way through the growing mass of colonials, forty to fifty on a quick count. The soldiers surrounded him and started jabbing with the barrel end of their muskets to drive off those nearest. When the fallen sentry staggered to his feet, he saw more colonials coming in from all sides. "Fight 'em off men!" he heard Preston roar.

His head spun around as the sound of the first musket cracked the air, followed by a flurry of shots. The astonished attackers froze, and then fell back in frantic retreat. There were one or two more explosions as the escaping men melted into the side streets, desperate to get out of harm's way. All that was left were the exhausted soldiers and the bodies on the ground. It was most strangely quiet. A moan punctuated the air when one stalwart man came back to pull a friend's wounded body into a nearby alley. "That was close," the sentry thought, wiping the snow from his face. "They meant to kill me for sure."

◆ ◆ ◆

The engraver studied the drawings mounted on the wall of his shop, then leaned over the work on the table before him. It was an almost perfect match. He carefully finished carving the letters "eet" to complete the banner along the top of the engraving, "The Bloody Massacre Perpetrated on King Street." Then he waved over the colorist, Christian Remick. Good man, Christian, one of the best in the business. Christian would do justice to his efforts. They'd been hard pressed to keep up with orders for the print ever since his drawing had been first shown.

The snowballs had magically disappeared from the scene. Red-coated soldiers shooting at unarmed civilians had become the theme. That should put the cat among the pigeons, Paul Revere thought. Then he smiled. Yes, it would do. It would do very well.

# Chapter 1

**Plimouth, Massachusetts—three years later.**

Patience settled back on the plump cushions of the sleek, private carriage. She held up Father's gift, a thick and most certainly dull, book of sermons for him to see. He nodded approvingly. She was astonished that he had left his church in the middle of the day to see her off. But, she thought peevishly, he had probably only wanted to deliver that last minute lecture. She could still hear him warning her in an ominous voice. "Do not stroll aimlessly around Boston, and," he had cleared his throat importantly, "never go anywhere without escort. Remember daughter, that city is nothing like our small Plimouth." She groaned to herself. The Reverend Samuel Burgess had strict rules about behavior. She quickly tucked the book between the seat and the inside carriage wall. With any luck, it could be soon forgotten.

Behind her mother, now trying to control Sam and Ben, the high-spirited youngest ones, she glimpsed Prudence and Jeremiah on the front porch of the parsonage. The newly engaged couple stood next to each other at an awkward, cold distance. She grinned happily at them. Prudence waved, but Jeremiah merely nodded stiffly. Patience concentrated hard on continuing to smile. How had her favorite sister become engaged to a stick like Jeremiah? He was earnest and sincere enough, to be sure, carefully following Father's example as a serious minister, but the man had no humor whatsoever. She shook her head decidedly. Not for her!

Without warning, the horses jumped to a quick start and she was jolted back against the headrest. She turned to peer quickly

out the open window. What had happened to Charity? Ah, there
she was, strategically setting herself against the backdrop of the
black walnut tree where any man passing by could easily see her.
She was supposed to be saying good-bye, for goodness sake.
Why did she have to act so foolishly? It was thoroughly irritating.
No matter that wide-set, crystal blue eyes and a perfectly straight
nose attracted a trail of admirers, her mirror-gazing vanity made
her most undesirable as a sister.

Patience pushed herself forward on the seat and smiled
halfheartedly at the beautiful Charity, who pouted and turned
away. Her jealousy at not being chosen to make the journey to the
Wentworths was plain. Patience chuckled to herself. Sometimes,
she thought, life is fair. She would have greatly preferred
inheriting Charity's blond prettiness instead of her own ugly red
hair and freckles, but perhaps this trip would even things out
somewhat. Besides, Anne Wentworth was *her* best friend, not
Charity's.

As the carriage picked up speed, Patience fumbled in her bag
to check for Anne's present, a container of her favorite beach
plum preserves. It was exactly where Mother had packed it. She
quickly craned her neck out the window and waved furiously at
her family. Father yelled a final "Godspeed," and Mother blew a
kiss. Sam and Ben began to run after her. "Have a great time at
the Wentworths. Write us about Boston," Sam yelled, his last
words stolen by the wind. Isaac, the Wentworth's reliable
coachman, snapped the reins smartly and the horses began to trot.
They turned the corner onto Main Street and her family
disappeared.

Patience pulled herself back inside the carriage and looked
around at the soft red leather. She had, of course, ridden with the
Wentworth family on numerous outings over the years, but it
seemed different to be alone in such luxury. She leaned back
against the upholstered rest, sure that she looked very grand as
she moved through the streets of Plimouth. Some of the
townspeople knew the fancy Wentworth coach and paid no
attention, but others strained to get a peek at the hidden passenger
within.

Perhaps she would pretend to be a great lady, being escorted to a ceremony of enormous importance. She spent a few moments contemplating how charming and gracious she would be in such circumstances, but as the carriage bumped along, jostling her considerably, her pretensions evaporated.

Minutes later the horses took up a steady pace on the Old Coast Road toward Boston. Sitting forward a bit, she had a good view of the marshes and duned beach on one side and the lush pine forests on the other.

From her vantage point, she caught a glimpse of several fishermen offshore. Although most of the fishing trade took place in large ships that went up toward the Grand Banks for weeks, or even months, there were still some who made their living by supplying the town with local catches. Many of the fishermen were Father's parishioners and often gave carefully wrapped packages of halibut and cod as gifts to the family. Patience wrinkled her nose at the thought. Venison tasted so much better.

Time went by slowly in the sun-baked carriage. Humidity settled in and, although it was still early, gave forecast of another scorching July day, The long-sleeved brown dress that Mother had insisted was protection against the dust was starting to cling to her slim body and perspiration began to bead on her forehead. She took a small rosewater-soaked cloth from her bag and ran it over her face, neck, and hands in a largely unsuccessful effort to feel cooler.

The occasional farmstead gave way to an increased number of houses and signaled the neighboring town of Kingston. Because Father had friends there, the family visited often, so she sat close to the window, hoping that someone would recognize her. But everyone was busy with daily work and the side streets were disappointingly empty.

She settled back, the thrill of the Boston visit absorbing her. Here she was, a small town minister's daughter, a perfectly ordinary person to whom nothing ever happened, starting off on a great adventure. She wiggled in her seat in eager anticipation. Boston was everything Plimouth was not: sprawling, bustling, and filled with interesting people.

She caught herself abruptly. What was the matter with her? She had forgotten again! She shook her head disgustedly. How could she not remember that this trip was only because of a dreadful accident, her best friend's accident, to be exact. She thought back, her cheeks red with embarrassment, as she remembered her last letter to Anne, how she had complained about boring Plimouth and about being forced to help sew Prudence's wedding clothes for hours at a time. "Just imagine," she had written, "how many stitches I've had to pull out." She had known Anne would sympathize, best friends always did. But her timing had been awful. Here she had been whining, no other word for it, at just the time Anne had taken that horrid fall down the church steps and broken her leg. And then, to make matters worse, she had sent the letter by way of that insufferable Thomas Warren, of all people, whom she had quite literally run into on Queen Street. Asking him to deliver her note had been a big mistake. Of course he had laughed and tugged her braids as if she were still a child for heaven's sake, instead of almost fifteen and a half. He thought he was so superior just because he went to Harvard! She shouldn't have given him the letter, but she had had no real choice. It was the fastest way to get it delivered.

When Master Wentworth's note arrived for her parents she had been properly ashamed about her grumbling. But almost instantly, shame had turned to excitement at the urgent request for her to come and keep Anne company for the months she would have to stay in bed. She felt guilty about that too. Why couldn't she have thought only of Anne?

Her parents had exclaimed over "that lovely Wentworth girl and her misfortune," and had immediately replied that Patience was available until the Christmas season, if that would help. And now here she was, little more than two weeks later, going further away than she had ever been in her life.

♦ ♦ ♦

The carriage continued its way through the coastline towns of Duxbury and Marshfield, then past the North River shipyards and Scituate. The hours seemed to crawl. Just as hunger pangs began to take hold, she noticed that the horses were slowing down. Looking outside, she saw that they were approaching another town, one that she had not seen before. Could this be Cohasset where they would stop to eat? She certainly hoped so.

The carriage turned off the main road and onto a bumpy side lane, then finally lurched to a stop. She looked out at a large brick building with a swinging wooden sign that read, "King's Three Bells Tavern." For those who could not read, it was also colorfully decorated with a picture of a king and three bells.

"Wait here, Miss," Isaac yelled in her general direction, as he hastened toward the tavern door. " I'll see ta th' Master's eatin' plans."

A few minutes later he returned and opened the carriage with a flourish.

"Take care o' th' step, Miss. 'Tis a mighty one," he fussed, holding out his hand to help her down. As she stretched for the first time in hours, she was grateful for his steady arm. They made their way slowly over the pebbled path to the tavern. The general noise of the place hushed to a murmur when Isaac pushed through the heavily timbered front door. They stood in the entrance, letting their eyes become accustomed to the darkness of the large front room. With few windows and little natural light, the place was pleasantly cooler than the carriage had been. The scent of brick oven-flamed venison and crisp biscuits fanned her appetite. Just as she was able to make out some shapes at the tables, Isaac led her firmly into a tiny parlor, complete with a miniature fireplace, reading chair, and small side table. Beyond the parlor she could see an even smaller room for washing up.

"You'll be served in here, Miss," Isaac said. "Freshen yerself and take yer ease. Th' servin' girl'll be in direct."

"But what about you, Isaac?" At home, their girl, Jenny, ate with the family.

"Don' ya fret none about me, Miss. I'll eat in th' tavern room wit' th' men. Th' servin' girl'll tell me when yer done wit' yer food."

On his way out, Isaac failed to shut the inside door completely, and although many of the sights Patience longed to see in the darkened front room were hidden, she could still hear the heated discussion that their entrance had interrupted. She immediately moved closer to the door.

"I'm tellin' ya good, them Lobsterbacks'll pauper us yet. Them British have already decided our tea'll pay fer their mistakes! Well, not me. There'll be no English tea in my house till that tax comes off!" the first man shouted.

"Right-o laddie," a second yelled, punctuating his words with the slam of a tankard on a wooden table. "Ah tol' the mistress, dump it all. We'll git use' ta liberty tea. It don't taste half bad!"

Someone snorted sarcastically. There were several answering chuckles. Suddenly the laughter was cut short by the unmistakable sound of heeled boots striding across the floor. A cultured voice rang out, "Ungrateful riffraff you are! The King protected us well from those murderous French and Indian enemies and continues to do so. And you don't think he's entitled to our support?"

"Enemies? They'un warn't aer enemies till them Lobsterbacks comed over and started shootin' at 'em!" ranted the first speaker. "Seems ta me we got aer enemies right here in th' midst o' us!"

There was a sudden unnerving silence. Patience tensed with fear. She had never heard men speak with such anger. She drew her shawl protectively around her shoulders and huddled against the wall, not daring to look out. Still no one spoke. Was there going to be a fight? That couldn't happen, could it? She had never seen men hit each other. Hot as it was, she began to shiver. Isaac was out there. Would he be all right? Finally, a strident female voice sliced through the awful quiet.

"Aye, come on gents. Easy does it. How 'bout 'nother round o' ale. That young lady in the next room wants to eat her meal peaceable-like. Hard ta, what wit' all th' yellin'."

No one answered. No one said anything. Finally Patience heard the sound of a pair of booted heels retreating, followed by the slam of a door.

"Them tight Loyalist breeches sure makes them walk funny," someone snickered. Loud laughter and additional insults eased the tension back into a general hum of conversation. continued. Patience took a deep breath and stared nervously through the sliver of the open door. The muffled sounds of male voices and occasional laughter continued. She let out the deep breath she had been holding, and was suddenly extremely hungry. She ran to the basin, washed up quickly, and sat expectantly in the reading chair. There was a sharp knock. A young girl, dressed in a low cut top that showed some of her shoulders and even part of her bosom, edged around the door. Seeing Patience waiting, she marched in with a broad smile on her face.

"Hallo, Miss. Ma name's Tilda. What'll it be today?"

Patience stared at her blankly, then felt her cheeks grow hot. She had never considered that she would be given a choice of food. She had no idea what to ask for. The serving girl came to her rescue. "How 'bout shepherd's pie? It's real fine."

Patience nodded, her embarrassment easing. Tilda departed to fetch the pie. Patience stood, stretched again, and began to amble around the small room. She wound up directly behind the door that Tilda had most considerately left ajar, just in time to overhear Isaac speaking softly. She leaned forward as far as she could without being seen.

"Well, in Boston," he began, aware that he was commanding instant attention, "we think that if we don't buy that tea stuff when it comes from them Brits, they'll have to send it back to where it comed from."

"Do them rich folk drink that Brit tea?"

"Well some do . . ." At that moment Tilda's voice rang out from a place near the door.

"Watch them hands, man. Mine are full a' hot food! Ya wouldn' wan' it fallin' on yer lap, now would ya?"

Patience quickly took her seat just as Tilda shouldered in with a tray of steaming meat and onion pie, as well as chunks of bread, and an enormous baked apple. Patience stared at the huge portion being set before her. Tilda winked and whipped back through the door, closing it firmly behind her. With nothing further to be heard from the main room, Patience devoured the food as if it were to be her final meal.

True to his word, as soon as her dishes had been cleared away, and she had again washed up and brushed her hair, Isaac knocked.

They retraced their path through the front of the tavern, and this time, she deliberately slowed her steps to get a better look. Enormous brick fireplaces filled with hunks of roasts churning lazily over sizzling embers faced each other from opposite ends of the room. No one but the unfortunate cook's boys came within ten feet of the smoky heat. Long wooden tables and chairs were scattered throughout the rest of the space where men crowded around talking and joking loudly. She saw Tilda laughing with two of them; one even had his arm around her waist. The trio quieted as they watched her walk by. No longer anxious about a possible fight, she was eager to see as much as she could and deliberately dragged her footsteps, but Isaac propelled her emphatically forward out the front door and into the carriage.

The hearty meal made Patience sleepy. She leaned back against the tufted headrest, intending to close her eyes for only a short time.

A hard jolt woke her from an unexpectedly long nap. Looking out she saw in the distance a town larger than she could ever have imagined. This must be it, she thought. What else could be so huge, so magnificent? The outline of buildings stretched for miles against the afternoon sun. She stared in awe. The horses slowed to a walk and the carriage lumbered across a natural causeway. Ahead, an imposing gate stood open. She remembered Anne saying that when you passed through a gate, you were actually in Boston.

They plunged onward into the noise and jumble of the city, past elegant brick buildings and taverns with their swinging picture signs. There were so many carriages on the streets that Isaac was often forced to stop, sometimes rather abruptly, to allow others to pass. Knowing that she should sit back against the seat and stare straight ahead in "a proper ladylike manner," as Charity had instructed, she was nonetheless unable to prevent herself from inching forward to the window. It seemed to her that there were more people on one Boston street than in all of Plimouth. They were everywhere. Gentlemen, dressed in handsome waistcoats and slim breeches, some even wearing powdered wigs, walked with ladies in daytime dresses that were fancier than her Sunday best. She felt qualms about the simple clothes packed away in her trunk. Would Anne be embarrassed? Unconsciously she tried to tuck back the wisps of curly hair that had escaped from the knot at the back of her neck.

Soon the coach left the business area and turned north toward the water, where smells of the hot city and the ocean mixed together, then past warehouses and neighboring large homes in close proximity to the wharves. Anne had said that men like her father, the shipbuilders and merchants of Boston, liked to live close to their businesses.

Patience had heard that not too long ago British soldiers stationed in the city had been assigned to housing in private homes, perhaps even some of these. As she remembered from eavesdropping on Father and Master Kimball, the owners of the houses had not been given a choice in the matter. She had never really thought about it at the time, but now knew instantly that she would not have liked a stranger living in her home.

Feeling the carriage slow down, she stared spellbound as they approached a large and imposing brick house, precisely edged with formal gardens. It was a full three stories high, with wide stone steps leading to highly polished wooden front doors.

Isaac guided the horses up the drive that circled around in front of the entrance. Near the steps, he pulled authoritatively on the reins. "Whoa, there." Even before the animals had obeyed completely, the house doors opened and a man dressed in a gray uniform ran nimbly down the steps. He pulled open the carriage door and offered his hand to help her down.

"Good afternoon, Miss Patience. My name is Henry. Welcome to the Wentworth home."

Patience took Henry's outstretched hand and climbed stiffly out of the coach, trying to move her legs without stumbling. Nodding in the general direction of the house, Henry said, "Lily will take you to your room first. As soon as you've had a few minutes, the Wentworths will meet you in Miss Anne's room."

A smiling, chubby girl, looking to be about Patience's age, with skin the color of mahogany, finally appeared in the doorway and rushed down the steps to take the small bag and carry it into the house. Patience followed. Henry stood back, looking perturbed at Lily's late arrival. Isaac, weary from the drive, struggled alone to pull the heavy trunk from the top of the carriage, and was finally successful. Henry, not seeing a footman, sighed resignedly, and helped Isaac carry her baggage into the center hall.

Patience stopped abruptly in the entry passage, the men backing up behind her. The entrance was a room all by itself, a complete two floors tall. At the far end was a curved staircase with brass rails on each step, holding the plush ruby red carpet in place. This was surely the grandest home she had ever seen. Immense twin sideboards, both bright with lemon oil, stood side by side, and gilded mirrors, looking as though they had been transported from English castles, were hung everywhere. Even Master Lancaster's house, and he the richest merchant in all of Plimouth, could not compare to this.

"Miss Patience," Henry began, a certain exasperated note overlaying his proper diction. Suddenly remembering that Henry and Isaac had their hands full with her extremely heavy trunk, she followed Lily quickly up the stairs. She was led to a guest bedchamber on the second floor that was twice as large as the one she shared with her sisters. The tall bed was covered with an embroidered canopy that matched its lavender bedcovers.

"Your bedchamber connects through that door," Henry nodded his head to the left, as he let go of his end of the trunk and Isaac followed with obvious relief, "to Miss Anne's. Lily will help you and then take you to the Wentworths."

Directions completed, Henry and Isaac left, and Lily began to pour hot water into the porcelain basin. Having someone wait on her was new for Patience and she felt uncomfortable. But within minutes, the dust from the trip had been washed away. She knocked eagerly on the door to the adjoining room.

Pushing it open in answer to Master Wentworth's loud, "Please enter," she saw Anne at once. Her best friend lay in a four-poster bed large enough to have dwarfed a less grand room. Her right leg was held high in the air by pulleys and rope. Her long blond hair curled damply around her shoulders and her face ("the face of an angel," according to Patience's brother Sam), was pale and pinched. Patience ran quickly to the side of the bed.

Anne's face broke into a radiant grin, the strain disappearing in a flash. "Patience, Patience! At last you're finally here!"

Anne's parents looked on contentedly as the girls, talking and laughing at the same time, hugged each other enthusiastically.

After a moment, Patience remembered her manners and rushed to greet the Wentworths. Master Wentworth, a tall imposing man with silver hair and a granite jaw, took both her hands, squeezing them slightly in his powerful grip. "Patience, it's wonderful to see you again. We are grateful to your parents for allowing you to spend this time with Anne."

Mistress Wentworth, considered shy and delicate by those who did not know her well, moved away from her husband's side. She smiled warmly and kissed Patience's cheek. Patience recited the greetings from her parents. Everyone talked politely about Prudence's wedding, Reverend Burgess' expanding parish, and the difficult summer temperatures of Boston and Plimouth.

Finally Mistress Wentworth cleared her throat delicately and looked up at her husband. "Dear, it's almost time to leave for the Governor's house."

Master Wentworth's face clouded. "I had forgotten. Must we go? We've barely had time to greet our guest."

"Now dear," Mistress Wentworth began.

"Oh Madam, don't look at me like that. I know we have to, just don't expect me to like it." Scarcely restraining his impatience, he nodded to the girls, then turned on his heel and marched out of the bedroom. He was closely followed by his wife who repeated soothingly, "Now dear, now dear." Patience looked surprised, but Anne only shrugged at her father's outspoken irritation with the Governor, "Father doesn't speak like that around others, of course, but you are like family, Patience."

A few minutes later Lily arrived with a tray of food, interrupting a discussion of Patience's boredom with Prudence's wedding plans. "Have you met Lily yet?" Anne asked.

When Patience nodded, Anne continued, "Lily is a blessing. She has been the only one in whom I can really confide." She smiled impishly, "Now I will have you too." Lily moved a small table over to Anne's bed and set it with the supper. Her task completed, she exchanged glances with Anne and slipped out the door.

For just a moment Patience sensed that some unspoken word had passed between them, but as Anne continued to press for details of the wedding, Patience's curiosity faded and she lost the chance to ask.

The evening passed quickly, and before long Patience was trying hard to conceal her yawns. Anne noticed immediately. "It's getting late and we're both tired. Why don't we continue talking at breakfast? There is so much that I want to tell you before my friends come by."

"I think you may be right," Patience laughed. "I seem unable to keep my eyes open, much less an interesting thought in my head."

That night, for the first time in a long time, she fell asleep as soon as her head touched the pillow.

# Chapter 2

The next morning Patience bounced out of bed in a sunlit room. The moment her feet touched the floor she was wide awake and eager to start her new life, the different and exciting one she intended to have. Lily had unpacked the battered traveling trunk, carefully hanging its meager contents in the large, ornate wardrobe. The extent of her belongings was not much more than that of a serving girl, making the decision about what to wear a quick one. She noticed that the chosen day dress had the tiniest tear near the hem where her foot had caught as she dashed to grab one of her brothers. She had forgotten to mend it and now hoped that it would go unnoticed. She dressed hurriedly, looking around the fancy bedchamber as she tied and patted and set herself to order. She brushed her hand lightly against the black walnut furniture. Its shine, polished to perfection by a succession of attentive servants, reflected back her excited face like a mirror. Mother had always said she would be happy with her curly hair and green eyes as she got older. She doubted that now. All she could see was that terrible color red.

She walked across the room and knocked lightly on the connecting door, hesitant to barge in until she was sure that Anne was awake.

There was a muffled response as she slowly opened the door. "Oh, I'd hoped you were up. What can I do to help?" Her eyes traveled over the lavish furnishings, settling briefly on the yellow satin draperies and matching bed linen. Anne was propped up against a vast array of embroidered pillows, already dressed in a day chemise with her hair neatly brushed.

"Oh dear, I thought that I could help you get dressed. Am I late?"

"Patience, Patience, please don't fuss." The familiar lilt in Anne's voice was overlaid with fatigue. The night before had been a restless one. "You are not here to dress me or wait on me. I have too many people hovering about as it is. What I truly need from you is just to listen and talk and . . . and . . . be here. It's been so tiresome having to stay in my room for so long."

"But that's no work," Patience immediately protested with a smile, thinking of Charity sulking back in Plimouth. "That will be much too easy. I thought I'd be able to do things for you."

"You can do things, lots of things. There are many places you can go for me. But first of all, I need you to treat me just like you always do. I am so tired of everyone acting as if I were a fragile piece of glass that would break at the first touch." Anne's voice faltered for a moment, then she quickly went on. "Tell me more about everyone in Plimouth. This is the first year since I was a baby that I haven't been there for the summer. What do you have to wear for Prudence's wedding? Is it perfectly horrid?"

Patience pushed an overstuffed chair close to the bed and sank in the cushions. "You're so lucky to be spared a sister getting married. You would think it was the only thing happening in the world. She's concerned about every little detail, even the buttons on the bridesmaids' dresses. Can you imagine?"

"Charity sounds as excited as if she were to be the bride. Is she still breaking the heart of every male around?"

"Of course. You can't imagine how trying it is to be related to her." Patience stood up, and tossing her head theatrically, fluttered her eyelashes at the bedpost.

Anne groaned, then asked, "And how is our favorite, Sarah Morgan?"

Patience flounced back in the chair. "Would you believe she's already sewing for her hope chest? Even with no hope and no chest!" The girls giggled. Mimicking the superior ways of the snobbish Sarah Morgan had always been a favorite pastime.

"Isn't handwork dreadful," Anne said between laughs. "I believe Mother has quite given up on me. I overheard her tell Father that maybe I would be better suited to voice lessons. She has conveniently forgotten how poorly I carry a tune."

Patience giggled again, picturing Anne somberly singing off key before an unappreciative audience. She tried to regain her composure. "It is really a shame what our mothers must endure to make sure we reach marriageable with some skill in place. At least in our family, Prudence is taken care of." She paused, and then added in a disappointed tone, "Though I must admit that there doesn't seem to be much romance between her and Jeremiah. Why, I've never even seen them touch, except by accident of course."

Then, as if she had just remembered, she asked casually, "By the way, did you happen to meet someone named Thomas Warren a couple of weeks ago? He was going back to Cambridge from Plimouth and I asked him to deliver that last letter to you."

"He did come. But it was too soon after my accident for me to see anyone. I looked even worse than I do now, if you can believe it."

Patience's eyes immediately clouded with concern. Misreading the cause of her expression, Anne hastened to add, "Oh, but I'm sure he is quite fine. Mother was very impressed with him. She asked about all of you, of course, and what he was studying at Harvard. Mother said he is taking up the law. She felt that he would be good at it from the careful way he answered her questions."

Patience hurried to change the subject. After all, Thomas was simply a friend of Prudence and Charity. In fact he treated her only as an annoying younger sister. It would be much too embarrassing if Anne misunderstood.

"Oh no, I wasn't thinking of him. Just you. Was your accident very painful? Are you in pain now? Here I am chattering on when I should give you peace."

"No, no, please," Anne replied quickly. "I have had enough peace to last forever. At the beginning it was most uncomfortable, but now there is little pain to mention, only a bit when the doctor comes in to move my leg so that it can heal properly. He says I am lucky to be mending so well." She paused as if ready to say something, but then let her eyes drift to a gold locket that Patience was unconsciously twisting back and forth. "And was that a gift?" she hinted.

Patience blushed and dropped her hand. "Oh no, not like that. In fact, not at all. This," she touched the locket, "belongs to an old friend of the family's, Mistress Dunham." She paused, "Actually, it has a rather interesting history. You see, she was the wife of a sea captain and traveled with him to every wonderful place you can imagine, until he passed on. Unfortunately, Mistress Dunham has lately had a serious bout of illness and, even though we tell her she is looking well again, she seems to be trying to get everything in order." Patience leaned forward in the chair as she got caught up in the story. "It seems that when she was a child in Boston she had a best friend. Rather like you are to me, I should imagine." She smiled at Anne, "When she was ten or eleven, Mistress Dunham had to move to Plimouth and her friend, Amanda Case, gave her this locket to hold until they saw each other again. One thing led to another and they lost touch. Now that I'm in Boston, Mistress Dunham wants me to try to find Amanda and return the locket." She reached up and unsnapped the clasp. "Look," she said, moving inches from Anne, "look at the picture."

Anne peered at the painting. "Is it of them?" She laughed immediately. "How silly of me. Of course it is. It's beautiful. They look so young."

Patience sat back and closed the locket. She sighed, "Don't they though? All I know is that Mistress Dunham is anxious for me to try to find her friend. She thinks that Amanda's married name may be Canfield. I promised that I would do my best, but I don't even know where to begin looking for her!"

Anne grinned, "I do. You must ask Mother. She has so many friends in the city, someone will have heard of Amanda Case. In many ways, Boston is just a large small town."

"That would be—"

Anne, her cheeks showing a pronounced flush, broke in, "And I have something quite interesting to tell you too." She drew in her breath excitedly, "A secret. I have been waiting so anxiously for you to come. Only Lily knows." She stopped dramatically. "I have met someone special!" Patience looked wide-eyed at her.

Anne rushed on with a flood of information, sentences running into one another without pause. "He is most superior, an Englishman, the son of an earl. His name is Oliver Mansfield and he's an executive officer for the governor. We met at an afternoon tea at Governor Hutchinson's about six months ago." Her eyes sparkled with excitement. "I remember the party so clearly. It was horribly crowded. Everyone had decided to go just to be seen there. My friends and I were trying to avoid our parents and had found a place to sit that was out of the way. Oliver came over to join us. I'm sure he chose us because we were the only ones enjoying ourselves that afternoon. She stopped abruptly and looked off to a place far beyond Patience, for a minute lost in her own thoughts. Then she began again, more deliberately, her fingers twisting the lace coverlet. "I knew that Oliver was wonderful right from the start. And he seemed to feel the same about me. But we've had to go about seeing each other secretly."

She hesitated, "It is so strange in Boston now." She seemed puzzled. "Feelings about the British are becoming absolutely unfriendly. I remember a time not long ago when my father and the other businessmen here thought England's decisions were fine, and things like colonial taxes were just accepted. Now, because of the trouble about that colony representation business, even my own parents, who used to be so friendly with the governor, avoid him. Papa says Governor Hutchinson rarely seeks his advice now and even more rarely follows it. Because of my father, Oliver only comes here when he can mix in with my other friends and not be noticed by Papa."

Anne pleaded with Patience, "I'm not sure how those in Plimouth see England and the King, but here things are becoming more and more difficult. It's awkward when Oliver is at the house because everyone sees him as the Governor's special assistant. David Tremont, who always seems to be around, makes nasty comments about England. Despite David's horrible attitude, Oliver always behaves with dignity. He is all too aware of everyone's feelings. We have our quiet moments, but I can't be too obvious in my attentions toward him." Anne mimicked her father's stern voice, "David and his parents are old family friends and always welcome." She sighed unhappily.

"I've told the others that Oliver comes to pay the governor's respects. They know that Governor Hutchinson wishes to keep my Father's friendship, even though he won't listen to his advice. Chiefly, Father says, because our ships carry a lot of trade to and from Newfoundland and that somehow helps the English merchants. Why, Governor Hutchinson even tries to be polite to one of Father's friends, Master Adams, because he is well-connected, even though he is a member of that Caucus Club." Anne shrugged as if she had no understanding or interest in the governor's strategy.

"Please Patience, for my sake, try to be friendly to Oliver so that he'll feel more comfortable. Because my broken leg keeps me trapped here," Anne thumped angrily on her bed, "this is the only way we can see each other." She lay back and whispered, as if the long talk had tired her. "I really need your help."

Patience, not usually at a loss for words, did not know what to say. She knew almost nothing of colonial problems with England and had never heard of the Caucus Club. Although her own mother had been born in England, there had been little contact with that side of the family over the years. They had strongly disapproved of her mother's decision to marry a penniless colonial minister. It was true there had often been talk at home about what had been happening between England and her colonies, but Patience had thought of it as men's business. She now wished she had paid closer attention. Nonetheless, she was worried about Anne's secret. Did the Wentworths have any idea how involved her friendship with Oliver had become? For that matter, was Anne herself imagining a romance because she had nothing else to think about now?

"You know that I'll always help you, Anne, but can't you speak to your parents about Oliver? If he's as wonderful as you say, surely they would approve and allow you to see him more often."

"He's completely wonderful! It's only because of this English tea tax. It has caused the people here to lose all sense. Oliver says that the tax is just because the colonies have received all kinds of services from England. He says we're just being stubborn. But some people here are opposed to the Crown's right to tax us at all!" Her voice was pushed to the breaking point.

Patience became even more concerned, remembering that she was there to cheer Anne up. Now that looked to be nearly impossible. Anne took a deep breath and went on. "My father is being influenced by these men and lately has begun to express his displeasure with the King. Not to the Loyalists' faces, of course. He is too sensible for that. But he plans to move us to Scituate, away from their influence. He's already started to build our new house." A bitter tone crept into her voice. "Naturally, Mother agrees with him. Now, despite Oliver's fine character, Father says it is not wise to allow him 'free access' to our home. He can only slip in when my other friends are visiting."

Again Anne paused. Patience, by now completely alarmed, but trying to appear calm, twisted her fingers nervously. She felt torn. Did the Wentworths suspect what was happening? Was this one reason they had asked her to come? She searched anxiously for something helpful to say.

Before she had a chance to speak, there was a sharp rap on the door, followed by the immediate entrance of Anne's parents. Anne tried, only partially successfully, to look less distraught.

"It's good to see you are both up and ready for the day." Master Wentworth's voice was loud from having to shout over the noises of the shipyard.

"Yes," Mistress Wentworth agreed, her tone a soft contrast to her husband's. "We thought the journey may have tired you enough, Patience, to lie late in bed this morning."

Patience smiled, thinking of the luxury of the carriage ride. "For a minister's daughter, I did indeed lie in bed late. Why the sun was full up when I rose."

Anne laughed, "We keep different hours here than when we summer in Plimouth. You're early by Boston standards." Seeing Patience's embarrassed look, she quickly added, "But I am so glad to start the morning with your cheerful face. I am always awake early with this as company." She gestured to her leg.

Her mother immediately asked how she was feeling.

"Better for having Patience here," Anne said firmly. Mistress Wentworth squeezed her daughter's shoulder and kissed her lightly on the forehead. Both parents looked more at ease, sure that Patience's stay was all the comfort that Anne needed.

"Well now, Patience, I am sure you will wish to see some of Boston," Master Wentworth said. "The doctor insists on rest periods for Anne so she may rebuild her strength." He looked pointedly at his daughter, then back at Patience. "You can certainly use that time to investigate the city, escorted of course. There are certainly areas around the town that are safe to explore, provided that you do not go unattended. Shops too, of course. Lily is a sensible girl and will go with you. Or, better still, perhaps you'll become acquainted with some of Anne's friends who are familiar with these places and can provide you with company. Now, mind what I say in this matter." He looked sternly at Patience, who nodded vigorously in return.

He sighed and softened his tone, "It's been difficult here since that snowball business near Congress Street. Even three years later, the killing of those unarmed citizens is something England cannot live down." He shook his head again. "Just moving that troublemaking regiment away from Boston to Castle William was not good enough." He broke off briefly, then continued, putting an element of drama into his voice, "Feelings here are running high."

Patience tried hard to remember what she had heard about any killings in Boston. She recalled her father and Master Kimball talking about something like that several years before. Father had spoken in loud angry tones, which he never did. But before she had been able to pick up any of the details, Master Kimball had noticed her peeking around the corner of the parlor. She had been talked to sharply about eavesdropping.

Master Wentworth's voice broke into her thoughts. Turning to his wife, he said, "I'm worried about these latest street fights. They're happening much too frequently. Tempers are even worse since Parliament agreed to let that East India Company unload their tea without paying duty. What could they have been thinking!" He began to pace. "It's clear to me that we must move out of Boston to our new place in Scituate even more quickly and remain there, at least until matters are straightened out." Heedless of the look of dismay on Anne's face, he nodded absentmindedly toward the girls and marched decisively through the door.

Mistress Wentworth looked with concern at his retreating figure. "I worry so. He seems to carry the weight of all these problems on his shoulders. So many men rely on his advice in these difficult times. I truly hope that the move to the lovely North River will bring more peace to our lives."

Turning to the girls, she firmly changed the subject. "That's enough of that! Now this afternoon, Anne, your friends are visiting briefly to meet Patience. Perhaps she will wish to walk with them a bit while you are resting. Tomorrow Master Allen will be here in the morning—"

"Mother," Anne groaned, "can't we wait another day for the schoolmaster's lessons? I'm feeling a bit tired."

Mistress Wentworth smiled knowingly. "Yes, I'm sure you are dear, but I'm also sure that some time with Master Allen will not strain you too much. Two hours of daily study is what we promised Patience's parents."

Patience frowned. What did Mistress Wentworth mean? Two hours of studying what? She had thought she had convinced her parents she was too old for any more of Schoolmaster Barrow's plodding sermons. Her thoughts were interrupted by Mistress Wentworth, who deliberately ignored her daughter's stormy expression.

"In a little while, after you've settled in a bit, Patience, I will have a small gathering for you to meet the mothers of Anne's closest friends. But for now, you'll see Deirdre, Pamela, and Suzanna themselves this afternoon." She emphasized the last name with a wry smile.

Patience replied quickly, "Oh please, Mistress Wentworth, don't extend yourself so on my behalf. I shall be quite content in Anne's company."

"Nonsense," she replied. "I am looking forward to the challenge of turning this bedchamber into a parlor." She looked around the room, as if to confirm her plans, nodded happily to the girls, and sailed out the door.

Anne laughed. "By the time Mother reaches the landing, she'll have everything including the flowers figured out. She will even have found a way to be gracious to Suzanna's mother, that insufferable Mistress Balfour."

Patience was surprised at Anne's tone. At home, they were never allowed to speak of anyone that way, certainly not an adult. Anne caught sight of her expression.

"Mistress Balfour's husband is a London mercantilist who came here to make advantageous business contacts. Mistress Balfour herself is forever going on about having to live here in the colonies, as if we were completely uncivilized. Suzanna is not a particular friend of mine, in spite of what Mother thinks. She is, in fact, a flirt." Anne made the last statement with such a tone of disapproval in her voice that Patience wondered with whom Suzanna flirted.

"Then why do you invite them?"

"Father says it is not smart to ignore such people right now. Mistress Balfour is happy to be included, and she gossips."

"But surely you don't . . ."

"Oh we never encourage her," Anne replied in an offhand way. "She just goes on, gushing about all kinds of things. You'll see how she is." This time Patience kept silent, thinking that indeed things were done differently in Boston. Many a night she had spent on her knees praying for the Lord's forgiveness because she had repeated something she had overheard. Reverend Burgess strongly disapproved of gossip.

Anne continued, "Deirdre Foster is my best friend, except for you, of course, and Pamela Cotton is a friend too, although she's closer to Suzanna since I have had to stay in this bed. Deirdre's and Pamela's fathers are both importers, but Pamela's father has agreed to sell that tea the East India Company is sending us and Deirdre's has not. It has caused a split between them." Patience was not quite sure of the significance of that bit of information, but did not want to show how little she knew. She decided then and there to listen closely when English relations were discussed. But first . . .

"Who is Master Allen, and why are we to spend two hours a day studying?"

Anne made a face. "Can you believe my parents actually thought it would help the time go by faster if we were tutored?

Math, French, and Social Sciences for two whole hours. And your parents agreed it was a fine idea."

"I knew nothing about it. Naturally they would think it was a good idea. And, of course, they wouldn't think it worth mentioning," Patience groaned. "I hope they don't tell Charity. She'll just gloat."

♦ ♦ ♦

After a light midday meal, Patience went to change for the afternoon with Anne's friends. She put on a simple skirt and her second best chemise; its mended collar looked fine covered with some careful handwork. Brushing her long auburn hair vigorously, she collected the escaping curls and fastened them at the back of her neck, then knocked on the connecting door. She entered the room as Lily was pulling a lovely bed jacket down around Anne's waist. Patience exclaimed over the cleverness of the embroidery, but Anne simply shrugged,

"It's from England, although I do think the Irish do the stitching. Mother brought several so I'll feel dressed up, even in bed." She looked carefully at Patience and added, "You look lovely." In truth, Patience's high color and burnished red hair made her look vibrantly alive. Anne knew that many would be surprised at the good looks of the Plimouth minister's daughter.

Soon thereafter, with Lily standing quietly in the background, Anne's friends came to call, sauntering up the stairs to the bedchamber in twos and threes, joking and teasing each other all the while. Patience was introduced and concentrated hard on keeping the names of at least Anne's closest friends straight in her head. Deirdre was quietly pretty, with lustrous raven hair coiled at the nape of her neck. Her dark eyes sparkled with amusement. She arrived with Pamela, who was quite plain looking, but beautifully dressed, as if her invitation had been to the governor's mansion. Standing beside Deirdre, Pamela seemed all bones and angles, with cheeks so bright they could have been dipped in a paint pot. Both girls stayed close to Anne's bed, bringing her up to date on their latest adventures. The flirtatious Suzanna had not yet made an appearance, but there were a number of young men in the room, more than a few of whom seemed to Patience worthy of getting to know better. One in particular, David Tremont, stood out, maybe because Anne had already mentioned him. He would have been quite handsome had he smiled, but his brooding dark looks, often directed toward the doorway, made her uneasy.

"Here's Suzanna Balfour," Deirdre whispered, as a young woman in red paused, then swept into the room. Suzanna was a presence. Tall and aristocratic-looking, she had long dark brown hair curled in ringlets in the latest European style and an obviously well set off figure, shown to its best advantage by a plunging neckline that would indeed have raised the eyebrows of Patience's mother. Anne called her over.

"Suzanna, please say hello to my friend Patience. She has been nice enough to come keep me company while my leg mends." Suzanne sauntered over to the bed and extended her hand like a queen to a subject.

"You're that minister's daughter from Plimouth. Lovely to meet you." She looked around. "Anne, is that Lucas over there?" Without waiting for an answer, she flitted off to tap the back of the identified Lucas with her fan.

Anne and Deirdre looked irritated at her rude behavior, but Pamela trailed after Suzanna. "Your dress is so lovely. And that necklace, is it garnets?"

Just then there was a slight commotion at the entrance. From the light in Anne's eyes, it was apparent that Oliver Mansfield had arrived. He, too, paused in the doorway as David stalked over to him. Patience could see immediately why Anne was attracted to the Englishman. Of medium build, he carried himself with a sense of importance. His blond hair, tied back at his neck, curled appealingly around his shoulders and his handsome features and coal black eyes were arresting. David reached him before Oliver could set foot in the room. Oliver frowned as he was waylaid. Patience was not close enough to overhear the conversation, but even from a distance, could tell that the tone was unpleasant. As she automatically moved toward them to see if things could be smoothed over, David, a scowl cemented on his face, left abruptly. Oliver came immediately to the bedside. Lily slid over to leave him room. The color rose in Anne's cheeks and her eyes sparkled as she motioned to Patience. Introductions were made and Oliver smiled kindly, but distantly, when Anne explained how Patience came to be in Boston. He paid closer attention, however, when Anne mentioned that Patience would be seeing the city with Lily each day while she had to rest.

"I do hope to see you on your walks, Miss Burgess," Oliver said earnestly. "My living quarters are not too distant, probably near many shops you may have an interest in visiting. Perhaps you and Lily will pass by."

At first Patience was surprised by his sudden friendliness. Then, without too much effort, she recognized the suggestion for what it was: a way to establish her as a go-between for Anne and Oliver. They had just found a way to send their secret messages.

Before Oliver could say anything further, Suzanna strode purposefully over to them and, ignoring both Patience and Anne, focused her attention on the handsome young man between them. "Oh Oliver, at last the chance to hear the sensible view of things. What was that horrid David Tremont carrying on about anyway?"

"Now Suzanna," Oliver began, his attention diverted, "you know we must ignore much of what David says. He considers everything that goes wrong to be England's fault. He has always held his friend's death against us. Crispus Attucks was the cause of his own death and all the rest of the snowball trouble on Congress Street, but David will never accept that."

As Oliver talked, Suzanna slipped her arm possessively through his and led him away from the bed, laughing animatedly at some remark he made. Anne's eyes flashed angrily for a moment, then she quickly looked exhausted. Deirdre was close enough to notice. "Are you feeling tired?"

"A bit," Anne admitted reluctantly, "but I hate to have everyone leave."

"Well then, we shall just have to come back soon. Everyone knows I have promised your mother that we'll stay only a short time when we come. We want to be sure that we remain welcome." Lily started to guide the group smoothly toward the hall.

Suzanna, keeping Oliver firmly in tow on the other side of the room, waved gaily toward Anne, "Take care, dear. We'll all see you again soon." Suddenly remembering her manners, she added, "It was lovely meeting you, ah . . . ah . . . Patience." She flashed a brilliant smile at having successfully remembered Patience's name, and sashayed elegantly through the door. Oliver gave Anne a half-hearted salute and followed close behind.

Deirdre was last. She squeezed Anne's hand warmly and smiled at Patience, "Perhaps you'll let me share a walk with you this afternoon. I'd like to show you around, as I am sure Anne would if she were able."

"That would be most kind," Anne answered before Patience had a chance to refuse. "I fear she'll become quickly bored with the quiet afternoons my parents enforce."

Patience shook her head, sure that would never be true, but Deirdre decided firmly, "It's not often I get a chance to show off Boston. I'll find Lily and meet you at the front door."

Patience quickly brushed her hair and tied on a bonnet. She had seen the tired lines in Anne's face and knew that Suzanna's possessive behavior with Oliver was probably the cause. She had instinctively disliked Suzanna and been tempted to speak sharply to her. But, for once, she had held her tongue, knowing it would only make everything worse. She walked back to Anne's room and helped Deirdre and Lily close the curtains so that Anne could rest.

◆ ◆ ◆

Patience and Deirdre were soon off down tree-lined Salem Street. The homes there, mansions by anyone's standards, stood majestically, surrounded by formal gardens. Deirdre pointed out one house in particular perched among brilliant yellow and gold day lilies massed by the hundreds. "Mistress Colman actually supervised the planting of each flower herself." She laughingly mimicked a snobbish voice, "She considers her garden of a most superior class." Patience grinned as she spied another home, facing east toward the sea, topped by a widow's walk, the haunt of an impatient wife waiting for the return of her seafaring husband. She knew that this street of lovely homes was grander than even Plimouth's Queen Street, and ownership of a Queen Street home was the major objective of many a Plimouth matron. She wondered what they all would think of the Boston mansions.

The girls followed Salem Street to its end where the path came to a stop facing an immense plot of open land right in the middle of the city. Deirdre explained that the original founders of Boston had set aside this land for the grazing of livestock. Nowadays, the bustling city used it as a public common. The path around the edges of the common was called the Mall. It was the usual place to be seen on a daily walk.

They ambled around part of the Mall, then took another route parallel to Salem Street, toward the busier section of the city. Deirdre nodded in passing to several people whom she knew but, intent on her job as guide, did not stop to chat. She pointed out several taverns and private homes where Loyalists were known to gather, including the quarters where Oliver lived. Deirdre did not say anything specific about the Loyalists, but her expression hardened imperceptibly when she pointed out Master Cotton's large shop close by. Patience remembered that Master Cotton had agreed to sell the British tea, but Deirdre's father had refused to do so. Patience glanced at Deirdre's face. She was not smiling. It did not seem a good time to ask what choosing not to sell the British tea meant. As they were turning back toward Salem Street, Patience thought she saw a familiar figure. Two men were talking in an alley, and when one looked up, she thought—But no, perhaps she was wrong. Deirdre hurried her along and she couldn't be sure of the face.

Soon they returned to the Wentworths, walking back up the street with a bit less energy than they had shown when they started out. Deirdre waved a final good-bye as her carriage drove away and Patience rushed up the stairs to see Anne. Anne was eager to hear the first impressions of a city that, as she said, she "often took for granted."

The hour for supper soon arrived, and not long thereafter, Patience left to write to her family. Anne was happy to visit with her parents, who showed up at the door just as Patience was leaving.

Feeling the effects of the long afternoon, Patience walked slowly to her room and, although she knew that she should sit properly straight-backed at the writing desk, sprawled on the comfortable bed and began the letter.

*17 July 1773*

*Dear Father and Mother,*

*My trip to Boston in the Wentworth carriage was exciting and only a little bumpy. I have new admiration for those who must travel often in this way. Boston is a most interesting city, but I confess to you I already long for the serenity of Plimouth, if only a little.*

*You will be happy to know that the Wentworths have taken every precaution concerning my safety. They see that I have an escort when I go out, and I am being very obedient in this as I am aware of your views also. I met many of Anne's friends this afternoon (they often visit to cheer her up). One in particular, Deirdre Foster, was very kind to me, and took me walking to show me where to go for the things that Anne and I may need. Life is very different here. There seems to be much tension about English soldiers and taxes; I am trying to understand, but I have much to learn. I will keep up with my prayers and conduct myself in a manner that will bring your good opinion. Among all these strangers, I thought I saw a familiar face this afternoon, but I feel I must have been mistaken.*

*Tomorrow I will begin taking lessons with Anne's tutor, Master Allen. Anne has told me that you already know of this plan. It will seem strange to have a different teacher, after having Schoolmaster Barrows for so long. I must close now, dear parents, as it is becoming dark and I do not want to light a candle unnecessarily. Please tell all the family that I think of them often.*

*Your loving daughter,*
*Patience*

She sealed the letter, said her prayers, and slipped into bed. As she closed her eyes, her last thought drifted at the edge of consciousness. Why was she sure she had seen David Tremont partially hidden in the alley this afternoon? Why also was she sure he had seen her and pretended it was not so? And why, particularly, was she left with the impression that the person to whom he was speaking was none other than Plimouth's Thomas Warren?

# Chapter 3

Three weeks rushed by before Patience received an answer from her parents. The loops and swirls of her mother's familiar handwriting, describing perfectly ordinary everyday matters, carried her back swiftly to her town and family.

*1 August 1773*

*Dear Daughter:*

*We were pleased to receive your letter and hear that you are well. Disturbing news of Boston unrest has reached us and we continue to be concerned for your safety. We caution you again to take care when you must be out and about, and in no event to venture alone on the streets.*

*Here at home, Prudence and Jeremiah's marriage plans are progressing nicely. Mistress Dunham has felt well enough to join the sewing group at the parsonage and appears happy to be of help with the wedding quilt. Your letter was shared as we worked.*

*Our good friend Master Potter was summoned to jury duty and John Torrey, Esq. also. Master Potter's eldest son, Matthew, is paying court to Charity, who appears to be taking him more seriously than most of her other suitors. He is a hard-working, pleasant young man, almost done with his apprenticeship as a miller. We approve of his interest as he has a settling effect on Charity.*

*Samuel is coming to an age when he may join the town militia. The men drill several times a week on the green, with*

*Samuel and his young friends looking on. It is difficult to imagine why we need this preparation and what will come of it.*

*Daughter, be wary and stay close to the Wentworth home. Please write often so that we may be assured of your safety and convey our greetings to Anne and her parents. Our prayers are with you.*

> *Lovingly,*
> *Father and Mother*

Patience felt sharply homesick as she absorbed the letter. She had been gone almost a month and was surprised how much she missed her family, even, now that she considered it, Charity. Instead of remembering Plimouth as dull, she was beginning to see the town as a welcome refuge from the furor of Boston. It was different here. Matters small, as well as large, intensified too quickly in the city.

Anne, desperate to remain in touch with Oliver, had persuaded a most reluctant Patience to become a go-between, carrying messages to the handsome Englishman. Patience knew that Anne's parents would be furious if they found out, but she did it anyway. Lily had been enrolled as an enthusiastic ally. To cover the deliveries of Anne's secret letters, Patience and Lily had taken to walking daily around the part of the city considered proper for young ladies. But two days before, they had walked into trouble. Involved in talking about something of little importance, they had paid no attention to where they were. Rounding the corner near Withington Milliners, they had suddenly found themselves in the midst of a fearsome argument between some men who supported the Crown and others who did not. Everything seemed to have started with a debate about who had been on the narrow pathway first, but by the time she and Lily had come upon the scene, had turned into a pushing and shoving match. There had been loud insults of "Lobsterback supporters" on one side and "ungrateful tax cheaters" on the other, angry words that had sparked her memory of the tavern argument she had heard on her way to Boston. But this time, she and Lily had watched in horrified silence as a clerk, who had come from a nearby store to see what the shouting was about, had been kicked and knocked to the ground, striking his head on the corner of a carriage post. The fistfight had waged on around him, while he lay stunned across the path. Fortunately, in spite of the blood streaming down his face, the man had managed to struggle to his feet and stagger back to the safety of the shop. The girls had clung together, protected in a doorway, afraid to take a step, afraid that the fight would move toward them. Perhaps in answer to their frantic prayers, those with cooler heads had finally separated the angry men, but not before more punches had landed and faces been further bloodied. Other than the usual schoolboy tussles, Patience had never seen a real fight before. She could not remember ever having been that afraid in Plimouth. The violence had made her feel sick, but neither she nor Lily told anyone what they had seen.

The tenseness of the city seemed to be seeping into the Wentworth household. Oliver was becoming increasingly unwelcome there. Yesterday Master Wentworth had muttered sarcastically to those in hearing range, "What! Is he here again? Doesn't the governor have some task to keep that young man occupied?"

Patience wasn't sure if Anne's father was angry with Oliver because he saw a close friend of the Governor, always in his house, or simply because he saw a man paying a great deal of attention to his daughter. Whatever the reason, Patience was anxious each time Oliver visited and always breathed a sigh of relief when the men missed each other.

She glanced at her letter from home once more, folded it carefully to read again later, and walked upstairs to Anne's room, her skirts swishing against her ankles as she moved. She rapped softly on the door.

Downcast and clearly unhappy, Lily answered the knock. Patience immediately looked toward Anne. One glance at her friend's swollen eyes and tear-stained cheeks confirmed that something was indeed wrong.

"Oh, Patience, because of the horrible trouble here, my parents have decided to move to the new house in Scituate in

January before it is even finished." She suppressed a sob. "If we move so soon, I just know that I'll never see Oliver again!"

Patience moved quickly to sit on the edge of the bed. She was at a loss for words and instinctively knew that whatever she might say would be of little comfort. But she put her arm around Anne's shoulder, and tried her best to console her. "Please don't cry. You know that Oliver cares for you." She searched for something that would give a shred of hope. "He is sure to visit you in Scituate." She added encouragingly, "It's really not so very far away."

Anne continued to look miserable, her eyes rimmed with red. "It would look too suspicious if he came there. Then my parents would know for sure that I think of him as more than just a friend. Father is already making comments about how often Oliver visits. What am I to do?"

Patience's heart sank. She had no clever ideas and feebly offered her only suggestion, "Why don't you write Oliver about your parents' decision? Maybe he can think of a plan. Lily and I will bring him the note when we go to the draper's shop this afternoon after lessons."

"Oh, no," Anne wailed, reminded of an additional reason to despair, "I had forgotten we had lessons again today. Another boring two hours talking about history! I don't care why the English went to war with the French or how poorly they are treating their colonies, as Master Allen continually implies. The men are the ones who make the decisions on these matters. Why must I take up my mind with those things? Besides," she added petulantly, "I am too old to still be in the schoolroom!"

Patience caught herself before she sighed aloud. It was easy to see that nothing would please Anne right now. With a lightness she did not feel, she tried to persuade her to think of something other than her separation from Oliver. "Yes, I know you're bored with studying, but it's a way to pass the time. Before Master Allen comes, I'll read you my mother's letter. Charity has a new, and maybe, serious suitor." She forced a laugh. "Wouldn't it be wonderful if both my sisters married at the same time. I confess, the thought of Charity's hand-me-downs make me shudder!" Anne managed a wan simile, knowing full well Charity's dresses, always too short and too frilly, looked miserable on Patience. Visibly trying to put aside her problems, she entered into a discussion on the relative merits of being an only child.

♦ ♦ ♦

A short time later Lily knocked, then opened Anne's door to reveal Schoolmaster Allen, standing tentatively behind her. As always, his hesitant appearance seemed to convey an apology for his presence in Anne's bedchamber. Patience could not help but compare him with Plimouth's Schoolmaster Barrows. Her old teacher was a short, untidy man who relied on his loud voice and the rod in his hand to get the necessary attention. His droning talks put his students to sleep on a regular basis. Schoolmaster Allen, however, was tall, with shoulders slightly hunched, as if he suffered from the weight of the schoolbooks he had to carry. He must have spent a good deal of time on his neat appearance. Not a stray hair was out of place, not an inkblot appeared on his white starched cuffs. Always speaking in a soft voice, his shy, crooked smile occasionally breaking through, he looked younger than his age. Anne thought that he looked "quite uninteresting, although I suppose some would find him handsome enough," but Patience did not agree. She sensed something mysterious and exciting about him.

The schoolmaster stepped into the room, placed his books and papers on the desk, and began the lesson without prelude.

"I believe that yesterday we were talking about the war between France and England," he began. "Why don't we continue with that today?" As he turned to pin up a large map, Anne glanced at Patience and rolled her eyes toward the ceiling.

"Anne, please review for us the immediate causes of England's most recent war with France."

Anne began a stumbling recital. "There was something about Indians, and wanting Canada, I guess."

The teacher quietly prodded her along. "How about the battle in Europe over the Austrian succession? The English and French were on opposite sides. You might add that as a reason. Do you think that was costly for the British?"

"I suppose so," came the disinterested answer.

"In what way?" The schoolmaster paused, and there was silence.

He continued questioning, "How do you think that King George is going to build up the treasury?"

"I really do not know," Anne mumbled, sighing audibly.

Realizing that he had exhausted her supply of answers, he turned to Patience.

"Patience, do you have any thoughts about this?"

"Well, I believe that the last taxes on the colonies were supposed to raise some of the funds."

"What do you think of England asking the colonies to contribute this money?"

Before Patience could reply, Anne cut in, her voice raised, "It is their right to tax us. After all, we are the King's subjects and must contribute to the support of the Crown. The King provides protection for all his colonies and we should be expected to help pay for the soldiers who give such protection."

At first Patience was surprised at how aggressively Anne spoke, but then she realized almost immediately that the words must be Oliver's. Anne was, in truth, defending his beliefs.

But the schoolmaster merely said, "Oh, do you really think so?" Then he added, almost as an afterthought, "The war has long been over. Why are the British troops still here at Castle William?"

Patience waited to see if Anne would answer, but her friend stared pointedly out the window instead. Patience quickly replied, "The Governor General says that it is in order to protect us from our enemies."

He pressed on, "And who are these enemies?"

She thought hard, but no one came to mind.

"Some say that it is to control us, rather than to protect us," the tutor offered.

Again Anne's attention returned to the discussion. "That is not true," she said, with an obviously angry edge in her voice.

He continued with his original thought as if she had not spoken, "Some say that the frightening snowball incident a few years ago between the soldiers and our Boston citizens, as well as the continued presence of the troops from England at Castle William, have made our relations with them worse."

Anne's face clouded with immediate irritation, but the teacher missed the obvious clues. Patience, however, did not, and tried to erase the edge from his remarks. "I am sure that there is something to be said on both sides," she inserted, attempting the soothing voice her mother always used to end the constant arguments between Samuel and Ben.

But Anne would not be deterred, saying insistently, "It is only those horrid men from the Sons of Liberty who are trying to stir up trouble. That miserable Caucus Club that tries to control the politics in the city does not speak for everyone. That Samuel Adams and those newspaper editors are just trying to blame the King for our own problems."

Master Allen's voice remained neutral, but his words were anything but. "Perhaps, but others are beginning to agree with his opinion. The high English taxes make it hard to save money for even food. Their current decision to favor the East India Tea Company over all others has been the final straw for many people."

In spite of his critical comments, he spoke in an almost disinterested tone. It was hard for Patience to believe that the obviously shy teacher truly believed what he said.

Perhaps the schoolmaster finally realized the extent of Anne's disagreement, or was at last warned by her expression that he had pressed enough. But for whatever reason, he wisely left the subject of British relations and started to review the latest French language exercises. Because French was a subject that Patience detested, the remainder of the lesson seemed to inch along until its conclusion.

♦ ♦ ♦

Lily arrived on the heels of the schoolmaster's eventual exit with a reminder of the afternoon tea that Mistress Wentworth had arranged with Anne's friends and their mothers. Anne tried hard to conceal her disappointment. Now there would be no time to write another letter to Oliver.

Patience, with Anne's direction and Lily's help, changed quickly into her best afternoon dress while the maids transformed the bedchamber into an intimate parlor. The footmen carried heavy, upholstered chairs from the dining room upstairs, and arrangements of roses and daisies were set everywhere. A crystal punch bowl filled with lemonade was placed on a lace-draped table in the center of the room. In a surprisingly short time the room was ready for guests and, if one ignored the bed, now adorned with an ornamental coverlet, was an excellent imitation of a salon.

Mistress Cotton and Pamela arrived first. It was hard to believe that the plump little lady, with a tightly curled wig upon her head, was actually Pamela's mother. She was almost as round as she was tall, and needed to angle herself gracelessly to enter the room. Her muslin dress, a sickly sea-green color, was not of the latest fashion, and ballooned unattractively around her. Looking about nearsightedly, she seemed ill at ease, quite unlike her elaborately dressed, self-confident daughter. Pamela again tried to overcome her plain looks by being clothed in the fanciest outfit imaginable: a pink satin gown, with flounces and crinkles of lace.

Mistress Cotton clutched her daughter's arm and moved forward awkwardly to greet her hostess, "Good afternoon, Mistress Wentworth, how kind of you to invite us. Oh my, I do hope that we are not too early. Oh dear, I do like to be punctual, but not too punctual, you understand."

"How nice to see you Edwina," Anne's mother responded graciously. "Here, please sit down next to me." She patted the neighboring pink chair. "It has been much too long since our last visit." She laughed, "I do believe that this is the first gathering that I have ever held in a bedchamber! Have you made the acquaintance of our daughter's good friend Patience Burgess from Plimouth?"

The sea-green muslin plopped atop the sturdy pink chair, covering it completely, and Mistress Cotton offered her hand,."No, no. I don't believe so. How nice to meet you, my dear. Pamela has told me you are to stay with Anne during this unfortunate time. How kind of you. My daughter has said such lovely things about you." She sat back, breathless after her spate of words, her head cocked to one side like a little wren, hopeful that she had made the proper remarks.

Patience made her own attempt at graciousness, "What a lovely dress, Mistress Cotton. Is it from Master Cotton's shop?"

Mistress Cotton laughed a tinkly little laugh. "Oh no, my dear, Hester is quite an accomplished seamstress and creates all our garments."

Hester? Who was Hester? Patience wondered to herself.

Mistress Cotton went on, "Hester's duties as my maid are often put aside in favor of her sewing responsibilities."

Patience was relieved that she had not asked who Hester was. There were no ladies' maids among her parents' circle of friends.

She was spared further conversation on the subject of dressmakers by the arrival of Deirdre and her mother. Mistress Foster, a close friend of the Wentworths, kissed Anne's mother warmly on both cheeks, and patted Anne on the shoulder. "Anne dear, you look worlds better to me. How are you?"

Anne smiled fondly at Mistress Foster. "Very well, thank you. And here is someone I want you to meet."

Mistress Foster's ready smile focused on Patience, "I know exactly who this lovely young lady is. Welcome to our city, Patience. We were so delighted to hear that you were to come to be with Anne, and now here you are."

Remembering her manners, Patience curtsied slightly. "Thank you, Mistress Foster. I am pleased to be here. It was very considerate of Deirdre to show me around when I first arrived. I was very appreciative."

Deirdre joined in, "We should walk out together again soon. I have just returned from a stay at my grandmother's house. Poor Grandmama had a spell of dizziness and required some help. But she is now fully recovered and I am back in Boston and this dreadful heat." She fanned herself enthusiastically.

"Deirdre, dear, be sure that you bring Patience to your father's shop on your next outing." Mistress Foster looked at Patience, "Master Foster has just received a shipment of lovely dimity from Europe. Deirdre has said that your sister is to wed. Perhaps the material would be useful; I'll ask that some be put aside for you. Sometimes it is difficult to have access to such cloth. Am I correct that she will be living in New Hampshire once she marries?"

Before Patience had a chance to answer, Suzanna and her mother swept into the room. It seemed as if tardiness was a particular habit of the Balfour women. Or perhaps they just desired being the center of attention that their lateness assured.

Mistress Balfour, an older edition of Suzanna, must have been a great beauty in her youth. Now, unfortunately, her appearance reflected her enjoyment of too many hearty meals. Even her fingers, each adorned with a ring, were swelled to capacity.

Suzanna took immediate charge of the conversation. "Are we late? Has anything interesting been said? Well, you'll just have to repeat it all." Pamela's mother giggled as Suzanna took a place in the center of the women.

Mistress Balfour puffed her way over to Mistress Wentworth. "I'm so sorry to be late, but it was just impossible to get the maids moving today. It must be this terrible heat. They've become lazier than ever."

Lily stood by the door looking expressionlessly at Mistress Balfour, absorbing the words to be repeated later to the other servants. Meanwhile, Mistress Balfour looked Patience up and down. "And this must be that minister's daughter from Plimouth. What a lovely opportunity for you to see Boston. You must be indebted to the Wentworths."

"How do you do, Mistress Balfour? I—"

Having completed her end of the social niceties, Mistress Balfour turned away from Patience and concentrated her limited attention on Mistress Wentworth. Trying to suppress a grin, Deirdre reached over and patted Patience's hand, whispering, "Pay her no mind. She is uninterested in all replies."

Soon the bedchamber buzzed with conversation. Patience listened rather than talked, trying to learn as much as she could about Boston. It may have been that the men made all the important decisions, but it was clear to her that these women helped spread word of them.

"Master Cotton has written to his dear friend, Lord Mansfield in London, and told him how unhappy some of the merchants are here with the coming shipments of tea. Master Cotton believes that a delegation of Loyalists should meet with the House of Lords to fully explain the unspeakably negative attitude of others, and to help King George with any unpleasantness here." Mistress Cotton preened. "Of course, Master Cotton would lead the delegation. I have made it perfectly clear that Pamela and I would accompany him to England if such a journey takes place. It really is time for Pamela to have her come-out in London."

Patience remembered hearing that the Cottons wanted to strengthen their ties with England and that Master Cotton was one of the Boston consignees specially delegated by the King as an agent for East India Company too. What was a specially delegated agent consignee? And why was there such a difference between merchants like Master Cotton who were so delegated and merchants like Master Foster who were not? Perhaps she should ask. But even as she was forming the question, the conversation turned another corner.

Mistress Balfour seized upon a kernel of information, "Lord Richard, Earl of Mansfield? Have you met his son, Oliver? He is here in Boston as an executive aide to the governor. Such a lovely young man and from such a fine family. I told Suzanna to invite him to dinner. I was introduced to his mother on my last stay in London and I wish to express my regards."

Anne looked sharply in Mistress Balfour's direction as she recognized a not so subtle interest in pairing Suzanna with Oliver. But Mistress Balfour paid no more attention to Anne than she did to anyone else and continued to ramble on.

"How is your new home in Scituate coming, Margaret? Master Balfour believes that your husband is wise to remove you and Anne from Boston at this time. There is such dissent among some of the rabble rousers over the coming shipments of tea." She fanned herself vigorously, "Matters are becoming quite unpleasant."

Mistress Foster spoke up quickly. "But it's been so difficult for the poor to buy provisions. Why, before the last repeal of taxes I knew of many a family who had to eat from the scraps of others in order to survive. Under such circumstances, it is surely unfair to protect one British company from bankruptcy."

Mistress Cotton looked confused. "Difficult? How can that be—"

Mistress Balfour cut her off. "The poor are just lazy, Marie. There's always work for those who seek it. And, as for the East India Tea Company—"

Mistress Wentworth broke in firmly, "Has anyone seen Paudlo's new exhibition? His use of color is breathtaking." Her comment was enough to send the discussion off in a safe direction.

The party was still going on late into the afternoon, past the customary departure time. But gradually the ladies noted the advancing hour and began to take their leave.

Shortly thereafter, Anne's mother left the girls in order to dress for another required appearance at the governor general's residence. Anne and Patience spent a quiet evening together, but their thoughts drifted apart. Anne's mind and heart were filled with Oliver, while Patience could not stop thinking about the growing problems over the English shipments of tea.

# Chapter 4

Friday dawned hot and humid. The draperies, the bedclothes, even the air, were all annoyingly damp. Despite the lack of a breeze, the tide-out mudflats scent of Boston Harbor extended its way to the normally impenetrable Salem Street. There was no doubt that the sultry end of August had arrived. Master Allen begged off from the day's lessons for "important business reasons," giving Anne and Patience an unexpectedly free morning. Anne's face lit with delight now she would have the chance to write Oliver about her father's plan to move to the new house by the first of the year. Patience and Lily would deliver the note sometime over the weekend.

Leaving Anne resting against a backdrop of newly starched and plumped pillows, humming to herself as she took quill in hand to pen her secret note, Patience drifted back to her own room and resolutely began to straighten up her belongings. "Tidying up," as Mother had referred to it, was hardly her favorite pastime.

As she folded the hand knit scarves neatly in the top drawer of the dresser, dutifully checking them for needed mending, her hand touched something wrapped in paper and stuffed in a corner of the bureau. Even without unfolding the paper, she could feel the hard curves of a small oval. It was Mistress Dunham's locket, put carefully away weeks before for safekeeping. She was instantly consumed with guilt. How could she have forgotten her promise to try to find Amanda Case? She had been so caught up in Anne's friendship with Oliver and the Boston debate about taxes and tea that the locket had completely slipped her mind. She was thoroughly disgusted with herself.

She marched determinedly to the back parlor where Mistress Wentworth began each day at her desk, organizing the daily household work. The small room was Patience's favorite place in the house. Although the ceilings were at least eight feet high and the woodwork noticeably ornate, the space retained a cozy charm. Now sunlight streamed through the windows, highlighting the yellow damask wall covering and warming the walnut desk set. The expanse was light and airy, an oasis from the early heat of the day.

"Excuse me, Mistress Wentworth," she began tentatively. "Would you have time to help me?"

Mistress Wentworth put aside her writing things, and looked up with a smile, "Of course, my dear."

Patience quickly blurted out her story. "My friend from home, Mistress Dunham, asked me to try to find someone whom she has not seen since childhood. You see, she grew up here in Boston with a close friend named Amanda Case." She held out the fragile locket, dangling it from outstretched fingers, "When Mistress Dunham left Boston ages and ages ago, Amanda gave her this locket. Now that Mistress Dunham is getting on in years, she is anxious to find out about her friend." She shrugged wordlessly, and then added hopefully, "She had heard that Amanda might have married a man by the name of Canfield. Anne said that you are acquainted with so many people in Boston, I was hoping…"

Anne's mother touched the locket gently. "Oh, my dear, I will certainly try to help you find out what happened to Mistress Case or Canfield, and might I say, Patience, that your undertaking is a most considerate one." She cleared her throat, "Let me see, since Mistress Dunham believes that her friend married a Canfield, let's start there. That name is not immediately familiar to me. Mmm, how old is your friend?"

"I have never asked her, of course, but she did say once that she moved to Plimouth in 1710."

"In 1710?" At Patience's nod, Mistress Wentworth paused again, and then came up with an idea. "I have a dear older friend whom I have known since I was a child. She has lived her entire life in Boston and seems to know absolutely everyone. Perhaps the name Case or Canfield is familiar to her. I have been meaning to call upon her and you have given me just the push I need to do so. I'll send a note this very morning."

Relieved that she had made a beginning toward keeping her word, Patience hugged Mistress Wentworth impulsively and skipped happily up the stairs to see if Anne had finished her letter. She peeked into the room in time to see Anne smiling to herself as she folded and sealed the note. Obviously just writing to Oliver was pleasure enough. Patience was momentarily envious. Despite her frequent protests, mostly to Charity, that she was totally uninterested in romance of any sort, she secretly worried that there would never be anyone for her. Perhaps it was only her imagination, but lately it seemed as if everyone had found someone to care about. A fleeting sense of loneliness descended.

She rapped on the doorjamb, and reminded Anne that Doctor Cobb, always referred to as "the good Doctor Cobb" by the household, would arrive later that morning. The doctor had said that he was so pleased with his young patient's progress that he would talk with the Wentworths about putting something portable around her leg, some device that would allow her to be out of bed. If all went well, Anne would at last be able to leave her room, even though she would still need help moving about.

"It will probably be a long appointment," Anne said, both nervous and excited about the examination. "Why don't you and Lily take a walk around the Mall now? It has started as such a warm day that it may be too hot to go out this afternoon."

Patience tried not to appear openly enthusiastic about the idea. Although lately the house seemed increasingly confining, she did not want to hurt Anne's feelings, "Oh, I don't know."

But Anne interrupted, "Please don't deny yourself the pleasure of being out simply because I must be here."

"Well, if you don't need me, perhaps a stroll would be a good idea. Would you like us to take the letter to Oliver now? Your parents always come with me to church services, so it might be difficult to get away this weekend."

"Yes, yes, definitely," Anne replied quickly, passing her the note. "I don't want to wait any longer to tell Oliver of my father's plans to move to Scituate sooner than we had expected."

Patience found Lily polishing the silver candlesticks in the dining room with great flair, if not efficiency. The maid was delighted to tell Henry that she had to accompany Miss Patience on an "important errand." Henry was somewhat less delighted, now that he had to reassign her polishing duties. He knew that the Mistress would soon be checking on those particular candlesticks, a wedding gift from a close relative who visited often. Continuing to look perturbed, he accompanied the girls to the door, closed it noisily, and watched from the adjoining window as they set off down the street for the house where Oliver lived.

Like most Englishmen stationed as government officials in the colonies, housing had been found for Oliver in the comfortable home of a wealthy Loyalist merchant. His two rooms were located on the far side of the Common, a pleasant walk from the Wentworths.

Even with the hot summer sun sparsely interrupted by shade, the street was still a better choice than being inside. The ocean breeze had finally started up and managed to stretch several blocks, gently ruffling the girls' light dresses. Cooler and more comfortable within minutes, Patience and Lily walked along quietly for a while, until the maid broke the silence.

"This weather surely reminds me of home," she began in a barely discernible accent. "Hot and drippin' it is 'most all summer."

Patience looked at her with surprise. She had never considered that Lily might have come from somewhere else. She had just assumed that she had always lived with the Wentworths.

"Where are you from?" she asked, at once interested.

"My mama is on a plantation near Charlestown. Leastways she used to be. I used to be there too. Once, the teacher who gave Anne and me lessons showed me where on a map. Charlestown is in Carolina."

Lily added the last statement proudly, pleased that she knew the exact location.

"I didn't know you had ever lived elsewhere. Have you been here long?"

"Seems like forever. Master Wentworth brought me here when I was real little. Anne and I are so close, I would never go back." She shook her head at some far off memory, but then murmured as an afterthought, "But I would like to see my mama again sometime."

Patience was silent. Except when Anne was upset, Lily seemed to be without a care in the world. She laughed and talked so much that Henry was forever speaking to her sternly about her "inappropriate" behavior. Patience had never given a thought to the possibility that there may have been anything sad in Lily's life.

"Do you have any brothers or sisters in Carolina?"

"I think so. I remember there were always babies around, but I'm not sure whose they were exactly."

Patience had never met anyone before who had lived on a plantation. She was not quite sure exactly what a plantation was like. As a matter of fact, she did not personally know anyone who had even visited the South. It seemed as though most of her Plimouth friends were born, lived, and died without ever leaving the town.

"Oh, look, here comes Master Oliver." Lily's plain black eyes lit with excitement. She was fond of saying that Oliver was the most handsome man she had ever seen.

"Hello, how nice to see you both." Oliver greeted them a trifle formally. His clipped British accent reminded Patience of home, although the long years in the colonies had warmed and smoothed the edges of her mother's speech. It was amazing that on such a hot day, Oliver still looked cool and elegant in his starched white ruffled shirt and immaculate black coat, the "uniform" of a governor's aide. Even his boots had been newly spit-shined. Scrubbed and polished, he appeared younger than his twenty-three years, closer to Anne's almost seventeen.

"How is Anne today?"

Patience could not resist teasing him. "Didn't you hear, Oliver? Anne has run off with a handsome French count and gone to Paris to live."

But Oliver did not give the expected laugh and seemed momentarily at a loss for words. She instantly regretted her attempt at fun and quickly said, "Oliver, I was just joking with you, of course. Anne is fine this morning. They're waiting for Doctor Cobb to come by. He's been so pleased with her recovery that within a month or so he may be able to put a support on her leg so that she can move around in an invalid chair."

Oliver's stiff expression disappeared immediately as his face broke into a broad grin. At once Patience was reminded of her brothers. Their faces lit up the same way when they discovered some new secret to share. Oliver certainly looked different when he smiled. Maybe he seemed so stiff because he was just shy.

"That is absolutely the best possible news, the best news of the day. Please tell Anne how happy I am for her. I understand from Suzanna that everyone is going to the Wentworths tomorrow." He added hopefully, "Perhaps Master Wentworth will not notice if I also slip in."

Oliver's wistfulness tugged at Patience's heart. She was sorry that he knew how Anne's father felt.

"Oh, I'm sure Anne will be delighted to see everyone, but especially you, Oliver." Then she remembered, "Oh goodness, I almost forgot my delivery. I don't make a very good messenger."

She handed him Anne's note and the young Englishman, with a wry grin, slipped it into his coat pocket, patting it in eager anticipation.

"I must depart, ladies. Please have a lovely day." Lily, delighted at being included, stood a bit taller, and she and Patience continued on their walk on the Mall.

A few minutes later, as they rounded the farthest corner of the Common, angry shouts shattered the quiet of the lazy, summer morning. Alarmed, the girls looked across the street to one of the narrow alleys where a number of men were shoving someone dressed in tattered work clothes. As Patience and Lily unconsciously drew closer, their eyes fixed on the argument, they could hear some of the angry exchange.

"Are ya darin' ta threaten the Crown?" one of the men yelled at the youth who appeared to be no older than Patience, "T'aint wise!"

Another pushed his way closer to the boy, "Ya' still wanna whine 'bout that tax?"

The boy shrank from the men and tried to reason with the leader, "But, sir, but sir," was all he could manage to say.

"Quiet!" a second man barked, forcing his prey against the side of a building. The boy's eyes darted desperately from side to side, looking for a way out.

Passersby stopped and joined in. "Hey, leave 'im alone!" one yelled. A worn looking woman from the other side of the street issued a rallying cry to the shop workers. "Them Loyalists are causin' trouble agin."

By now Patience and Lily were on the outskirts of a growing crowd, but in a good place to see clearly what was going on. Those around them began to push forward, their anger contagious. Out of the corner of her eye, Patience glimpsed David Tremont in front of the stationer's shop, looking furious, but prevented from getting closer by the number of those already there. The men closed in on their target as he tried to evaporate into one of the nearby doorways.

The leader jammed his finger against the boy's chest. "Yer talk of unfairness is treason! The Crown protects us with that tax money. I'll report ya ta' th' soldiers! Some time in jail'll change yer mind about a tea tax!"

Patience felt a surge of panic as the King's supporters circled the youth menacingly. Finally, men, and even a few women, elbowing to gain an advantage, angrily pushed into their midst to oppose them. Patience clutched Lily's hand tightly, and clung to the corner of the nearest building, determined not to be dragged into the trouble.

At the threat of jail, the boy found his tongue at last, "Sir, please, please, I'm not doin' nuthin'. I only said others can't compete with th' cheaper prices this tea'll fetch." He ended more confidently, "That's th' truth."

Patience looked around desperately. Over the heads of the crowd she saw Oliver running toward them from the opposite direction. Thank goodness! Oliver worked for the governor. He could reason with these bullies and protect the boy.

"Hold, there," Oliver yelled above the din as he shoved his way into the center of the crowd, "What goes on here?"

"Sir, sir—" the frightened youth began.

"You, keep quiet," Oliver retorted, glaring at him. He turned to the ringleader. "What happened?"

"That one threatened the tea coming from England." A blunt finger pointed at the youth.

Oliver grabbed the boy by the shoulders and shook him roughly. He snapped, "Do you know who I am? Governor Hutchinson's aide, that's who. You threatened the private property of the East India Company. That's the same as threatening the Crown. You could spend time in jail for that!"

Again the boy tried to defend himself. "But, sir, I didn' say nuthin' 'bout hurtin' th' tea!"

Before he could finish, Oliver, glancing apprehensively at the growing crowd, who were jostling each other and trading insults and curses, growled loudly, "I won't turn you in today, but be warned! Your loose tongue will surely land you in jail next time!" He pushed the frightened boy away. "Now be off at once!"

As the boy escaped down the street, looking anxiously over his shoulder, Oliver turned to those remaining and yelled harshly, "There is nothing more to be seen here. Go about your business."

Patience and Lily had been but two in a blur of many faces, and Oliver took no note of them as he marched off to the side of the street, trailed by the Loyalists. The crowd broke up slowly, with many mumbling angrily about restrictions on speaking one's mind.

Relieved that Oliver had not seen them, Patience pulled Lily along the side of the closest building. She was outraged that he had only listened to one side of the story. And he had used his authority to intimidate that poor boy. How could he have acted that way! People were right; the freedom to speak on the streets no longer existed!

As she and Lily began to retrace their steps back to the Mall, Patience's color high with suppressed indignation, a blurred movement caught her eye. David Tremont stood in the shadows, gesturing furiously to a man who, even on such a hot day, was wearing a hat pulled low, hiding his face. Something about the man was vaguely familiar, but her attention was drawn quickly to David, whose intense frustration was obvious. When she and Lily passed, David glanced at her, but did not speak.

Patience's anger barely eased during the walk home. Lily, visibly confused by what she had seen, did not say a word. At the bottom of the steps to the Wentworth house, Patience took a deep breath. "Lily, I don't think we need tell anyone what happened. It . . . it might upset them." Lily nodded in relief. She had no desire to tell "them" either. Neither mentioned the incident to Anne, who was only interested in whether her letter had been delivered. With considerable difficulty, Patience was able to speak lightly of the conversation with Oliver. Anne was delighted at the prospect of his afternoon visit. Her father would still be at the new shipyard on North River and there would be no danger that the paths of the two men in her life would cross.

The news from Doctor Cobb had been very encouraging. A brace to allow Anne to move about would indeed be placed on her leg within the next several weeks. Master Wentworth had ordered his men to complete an invalid chair for her.

"I will be able to stand on my own two feet, even if it is with help, just in time for my birthday in October. What a wonderful seventeenth birthday present!" Anne exclaimed joyously.

Her excitement was contagious and the incident in town was finally pushed to the back of Patience's mind, but not forgotten.

# Chapter 5

The August heat continued without a break, one steamy day after the next. On the last Tuesday before the end of the month Mistress Wentworth, seemingly unaffected by the dripping humidity, set out in the carriage immediately after the noon meal, leaving a message that the girls were not to dress for afternoon tea until she returned.

When the rumble of nearby wheels woke Patience from a nap, she parted the draperies, limp with moisture, and peered out the window. The Wentworth transport, streaked by the dust of the hot Boston streets, rolled up the drive, the horses lumbering along uncomfortably. Isaac, his hat askew, pulled the reins sharply, then lowered himself slowly from the top of the carriage and looped the strips of leather around the front post. Martin, the newest stable lad, rushed forward to hold the horses as Isaac opened the carriage door. The mistress of the house, looking as unruffled as she had three hours before, entered her home. Isaac disappeared momentarily into the carriage, then reappeared with a high stack of fancy ribboned boxes, and followed in her wake.

Patience splashed cool water on her face to erase the last remnants of her groggy sleep and, hearing Anne and her mother next door, pushed through the connecting door.

Mistress Wentworth and Isaac, who still bore his load, stood at the foot of the bed.

"Oh girls," Mistress Wentworth exclaimed excitedly, "I have had the most splendid afternoon, First, I stopped by Mistress Tremblay's. You remember her Anne, dear, she was Grandmother's closest friend." She smiled at Patience. "I had not seen her in ever so long and have lately renewed our acquaintance. The poor dear had not been to the dressmakers in absolutely months, and I offered to take her to Madame

Toussignant's shop. She was naturally pleased to be out. It is so difficult when one gets on in years. Anyway, while we were there, I found two perfectly lovely afternoon dresses that had been ordered by Mistress Richardson for her daughters before their unexpected June departure for England." She paused. "I must say I wonder what the reason. No one has heard of them since." The girls waited patiently while she considered a variety of possible answers. Having no success in solving the puzzle, she started again. "Poor Madame Toussignant had been left with the garments. Isaac, there is no need to hold onto those packages, just set them down." Isaac looked at her blankly, then slowly complied. She continued, "I have been looking for the perfect opportunity to celebrate Doctor Cobb's good news. The dresses were exactly right for you girls, so I purchased them on the spot. Then, of course, I needed underskirts and petticoats and shoes to match. Such a lovely time Mistress Tremblay and I had!" She clasped her hands together in satisfaction. "I do hope that everything will fit. Anne dear, your dress will be for the very first day that you leave this bed." She looked fondly at her daughter. "But for now, I have a new jacket for you to wear this afternoon."

She spoke without taking a substantial breath between sentences, as she lifted each box top in rapid succession while Isaac, looking considerably worn, stood as guardian of the packages. "It's here somewhere." The girls smiled at each other. Finally, in the last box, she came upon the new jacket. It was a pale blue, silk froth, trimmed richly with imported lace at the sleeves and neck; a color that would look especially fine with Anne's golden hair and blue eyes. She shook out nonexistent wrinkles and laid it across her daughter's lap. Anne was delighted, holding it up and fingering the cut lace happily.

Then, with a flourish, Mistress Wentworth unwrapped Anne's new afternoon dress. It was pink, with miniature roses embroidered throughout the material. The accessories matched perfectly, right down to the silk slippers. It was the most enchanting dress Patience had ever seen. Anne looked at the gown longingly and promised. "Soon, very soon. This is one dress that I'm ever so anxious to wear." Lily carefully spread the outfit over Anne's bed for a closer look. Mistress Wentworth drew a second dress slowly out of its package. She looked at

Patience, "My dear, you have been a true friend to my daughter. With you here, she is acting like herself again. Her Father and I would like you to have a small token of our thanks."

At first Patience saw just a mass of shimmering yellow silk - brilliant as the morning sunlight. Then the dress was held high and she had a full view. The bodice was cut low and folded tightly. Like Anne's dress, the neckline and sleeves were trimmed with lace, but this lace was dyed to match the silk material. The skirt had yards and yards of sunlit silk gathered with waistline bows. She was speechless. "But Mistress Wentworth," she began, "I really can't accept—"

"Quickly, quickly, girls." Mistress Wentworth interrupted, looking pleased with herself. She patted Patience's shoulder and refused to be drawn into further discussion. "There's little time before your friends come. I will send Martha. She and Lily can help you get ready." She departed in a flash, calling for her personal maid.

Patience tentatively touched the yellow material. Did this dress really belong to her? She had never seen anything so fragile.

Anne was delighted, "Oh, you'll look absolutely beautiful. Please let Mama do this for you; it gives her so much pleasure. We'll have Martha fix your hair. She does Mother's all the time for fancy parties." She giggled and her eyes danced mischievously, "We will surely irritate Suzanna with how well we look."

When put that way, Patience did not see how she could refuse. Soon the room was a sea of dresses, ribbons, and slips. Martha, in her acknowledged superior position as lady's maid to the mistress of the house, directed Lily and Becky, a thin little twelve-year-old in training, as they gradually brought order to the clothing chaos. Finally dressed, Patience, commanded not to look in the mirror until she was "done", sat in a straight back chair while Martha fussed with her hair.

Instead of the mirror she faced Anne, who sat propped against the headboard of the bed, offering suggestions.

Watching her direct the lady's maid, Patience realized that her best friend was indeed grown up, and for a moment remembered back to their first meeting at Plimouth beach when they were five and six, respectively. It seemed like such a long time ago. She recalled that she had been clamming near the rocks with her favorite stick and had been thoroughly muddy. She had looked up to see a blond, delicate creature in a slip of a summer dress walking barefoot on the sand. A man, Master Wentworth as it turned out, marched along behind her, carrying her shoes and blanket and a collection of slightly sandy shells.

She had known instantly that these were "summer people," because no one from town dressed that way for a walk on the beach.

Anne had smiled first, shyly, but the invitation had been enough for Patience to attach herself immediately. From that tentative beginning a fast friendship had been born. All that seemed a long time ago.

Anne looked so beautiful. The new blue jacket made her eyes seem almost violet. Patience knew that the price of such good looks was usually arrogance, but Anne seemed completely unaware of herself.

After what seemed like an eternity, Anne smiled with satisfaction, "Now you may look."

Trying to move without stumbling in the new shoes, Patience stood up slowly and stared into the full-length glass. Was that really her? The dress looked as if it had been made especially for her, cleverly tucked and revealing a slightly daring neckline. The flowing skirt was just high enough off the ground to allow the matching slippers to peek through. The dress had worked its magic. She looked five years older.

Instead of securing Patience's auburn hair tightly in back, Martha had allowed the natural curls to come forth and gently brush her shoulders with ringlets. Narrow yellow ribbons, looped in strategic places, held back some of the curls, in the best imitation of the latest European style.

Martha was very pleased with the outcome. "Now you look like a proper young lady," she pronounced with finality.

"You certainly do," Anne agreed, with a wink behind Martha's back.

Others soon echoed admiration for the maid's handiwork. David, who came into Anne's room with Deirdre, flashed Patience an appraising smile.

Deirdre thought that Patience looked splendid and said so often, but Pamela and Suzanna were only grudgingly complimentary, not at all pleased that a country girl could so easily take the attention that was rightfully theirs. On the other hand, the men were outrageously flattering, and Patience tried flirting from behind a borrowed lacy fan, as she had often seen Charity do. Enjoying the teasing, she thought that it might be quite pleasant to become better at it.

Eventually everyone broke into smaller groups for parlor games, while Lily served the punch. Anne and Oliver were soon deep in conversation in their own private world. When Patience passed nearby and overheard Oliver start to talk about what had happened at the Common, she deliberately moved closer to hear what he said.

"You wouldn't believe the trouble that no account boy caused. I realize that everyone is not like us, that some are less than intelligent in their opinions. But really, listening to disloyal ravings only inflames people." Oliver's words were projected carefully, pearls of wisdom being sent forth. He continued in his precise accent, which now grated on Patience's nerves. "Fortunately, the Loyalists there behaved in a calm and rational manner. I was very proud of the restraint shown after being confronted the way they were."

Patience could not believe her ears. That was not what had happened at all! How could he think such a thing! A threat to the Crown's right? Never! The boy was afraid and being bullied for speaking his mind.

It was outrageous, yet if she opened her mouth to retort, she would only say things that she could not take back. She moved away, gritting her teeth and swallowing her rising anger.

As she saw Anne gaze adoringly at Oliver, she suddenly realized that Master Wentworth had reason to worry about his daughter's interest in this English nobleman. She also knew that from now on she had better keep her opinions about the Crown to herself.

Deep in angry thought, she came close to bumping into David who was standing off by himself as usual. He murmured to her, "It would seem that Anne is becoming more interested in the King's point of view with each passing day. What did you think of what happened?"

His question startled her. She was torn between speaking frankly, telling him exactly what she thought of Oliver's behavior, and remaining loyally silent for Anne's sake.

She took a breath and avoided a choice by asking, "I saw you there. Why didn't you speak to me?"

David was immediately defensive, "I was busy with a friend." His face clouded with emotion. "You did not appear to be in need of any assistance. And I . . . I was too upset at the Loyalists to speak civilly with anyone."

"Yes," she said instantly, momentarily forgetting her allegiance to Anne. "I too, couldn't believe the way that poor boy was treated simply for saying what he did."

Both Patience and David had unconsciously lowered their voices, and now moved away from the others. David continued with barely restrained emotion. "Those who support the Crown are becoming worse in handling any opposition." He added bitterly, "And they have the power behind them. We are constantly reminded of the British troops at Castle William, able to be called out at a moment's notice. I had thought that Parliament and that idiot George were at least trying to resolve their differences with us after the murder of Crispus and the others during that foul snowball incident, but I was wrong. They had better beware. The Sons of Liberty will soon answer their insulting intolerance for our concerns."

"Even in Plimouth I've heard of the Sons of Liberty," Patience whispered, "but not a lot about them. Do you know anybody who is one?"

David answered swiftly, and a trifle sharply, "There are many reasons why a man wouldn't make his membership known." He looked at her intently, "Those abroad find ways to take revenge on others who don't fully support either their miserable opinions or their outrageous taxes."

It was obvious that David was trying hard to discourage her questions about the Sons of Liberty, but that only aroused her curiosity further. Seeing that she would gain nothing by continuing to push him for information, however, she let the matter drop. She would have to find out about them some other way.

Suzanna passed by on her way to Anne's bed. She came up behind Oliver, insistently taking his arm. Lacing her fingers securely with his, she tugged, "Come, Oliver. Let's all play a final game of whist together." Her demanding voice effectively ended all private conversations, "Anne won't mind if you join us, will you dear?" Anne clearly did mind and looked disgustedly at Patience as soon as Suzanna's head was turned. "Come, David, sit by Pamela," she continued authoritatively. "Patience probably hasn't learned to play yet. I'm sure that she'll be content to watch."

As even David moved obediently to the card table, Patience saw again how completely annoying Suzanna could be. Concerned with no one's opinion, Suzanna continued to manage the card players and ensured that the game lasted until Lily came to announce the arrival of the carriages.

Having promised Anne that she and Oliver would have a few minutes alone, Patience walked the others slowly down the stairs, playing up to Suzanna's vanity, involving her completely by asking about the pleating on her elegant blouse.

Mistress Wentworth waited by the front entrance while Lily and Becky passed out the light shawls. She spoke quietly to Patience under cover of the farewells, "Isn't Master Mansfield leaving? I do think it's time. Please tell him that the Balfour carriage will take him to his quarters if he wishes."

As slowly as she could decently obey, Patience went back upstairs to the bedchamber to convey the insistent request. A gentle knock on the door brought no response, so she pushed it open slightly, calling Anne's name.

Her gaze caught Anne and Oliver together. He was kneeling next to the bed, his arms intertwined with hers. Lips pressed together, they were oblivious to everything but one another. Patience stopped abruptly and shut the door immediately. She was startled and embarrassed at such affection. Anne's parents would certainly be angry if they knew. Anne and Oliver were not even engaged! Such things were just not allowed. She was relieved that she, and not Mistress Wentworth, had come upon them.

After a couple of tense moments, she rapped on the door again, this time much more sharply. Anne answered with forced gaiety, "Do come in. Oliver is looking for a book that I'm lending him." Patience pushed the door open.

Oliver stood next to the bed; both he and Anne looked flustered. Patience, hot-faced herself, recited Mistress Wentworth's message, while trying to avoid their eyes. Oliver left Anne's side reluctantly, tugging down the edge of his slightly wrinkled jacket, and marched down the stairs, without a book, to finally bid Mistress Wentworth farewell. He decided he was going to walk the short distance to his living quarters, he said. Mistress Wentworth closed the door firmly on him.

She turned to Patience. "Dear, I meant to tell you earlier of some wonderful news. My old friend Mistress Tremblay is indeed acquainted with Amanda Case. They both attended the Church of St. James as children, and later socialized as young women coming into society. Mistress Dunham was right. Amanda Case married Hollings Canfield. Mistress Tremblay tells me that Master Canfield has passed on and Mistress Canfield is now living with her daughter, who is married to one of our most prominent Boston attorneys. She is quite frail and Mistress Tremblay has not seen her in some time. But when I relayed the tale of the locket, she was intrigued and resolved to send her a note."

Patience clapped her hands in delight. She was thrilled at the prospect of meeting Mistress Dunham's childhood friend. When she slept that night, she dreamed of two young girls running on a beach, carefree and happy. As they played in the shallow water, she fancied she saw them looking up to spy a ship passing on the horizon. One of the girls pointed excitedly. They ran along the ocean's edge to keep the ship in sight as long as possible. In her dream, however, the faces of the girls were unclear. Who were they?

◆ ◆ ◆

The next day a slight breeze made Patience and Lily's walk to the drapers for new ribbons more comfortable. As they strolled along Park Street, Patience looked up and saw a familiar figure approaching. He was tall, with broad shoulders, unruly black hair, and a mischievous grin.

"Thomas! Thomas Warren, how are you?" she exclaimed, delighted to have someone from home appear so unexpectedly in her path.

Thomas, by this time close by, looked startled. He hesitated, "Patience, is that you? I barely recognized you. You look so different."

Patience was thrilled. He had treated her like such a child when she had last seen him in Plimouth that he deserved to be surprised. She decided to be as charming as she knew how. "Goodness, Thomas, it's been ever so long since we've seen each other," she said, fluttering her eyelashes, giving her best imitation of Suzanna.

Unfortunately, her flirtatious manner did not have quite the desired result. Thomas, reaching for a linen handkerchief, said with concern, "Have you something in your eye?"

Watching the failed attempt at charm, Lily laughed to herself, Goodness me, she surely doesn't have that right. Patience sighed in resignation. "No, I'm fine, Thomas. How nice to see you. How are your studies at Harvard coming?"

"Wonderfully," he answered, as the three of them moved to the side of the path where they would no longer be in the way of those hurrying along on more important matters. "I'm almost finished with my classroom work and am now clerking for a lawyer here in town. It was a most desirable position and a wonderful chance to learn twice as much real law as I do in my studies. Boston is definitely the place for a lawyer to be right now."

His face showed a contagious excitement. Patience murmured politely, but when she caught him looking at her with interest, her heart beat faster and she could feel her cheeks start to flush. Her eyes fell upon Lily and she realized that she had forgotten all about her and the errand to the drapers.

Looking toward the shop, Lily suggested, "Should I buy the ribbons? The store is only next door and I'll be back right quick."

"Yes, thank you, Lily, that'd be fine," she said, handing Lily her purse.

The maid slipped the purse over her wrist and was quickly, and importantly, on her way. Thomas continued to study Patience. "You don't look the same. What's different?"

She smiled, mysteriously she hoped, and answered slowly, "Nothing I know of." She carefully patted an imaginary stray curl into place.

Still looking slightly puzzled, he changed the subject. "I heard you were staying with the Wentworths. Have you been enjoying yourself?"

"It's been very interesting," she said cautiously, "much less quiet than life in Plimouth." She smiled to herself as she realized how diplomatic she was becoming. A few short months ago she would have blurted out not only every incident she had witnessed, but every thought and word as well.

"Really? How's your friend Anne doing now?"

"She's well, although naturally bored at having to stay in bed. Master Wentworth has tried to be helpful and has a tutor come in to give us lessons. I never thought I'd say this, but I'm actually enjoying the study. The tutor's very nice, certainly different from that self important Schoolmaster Barrows."

Thomas laughed, "I remember well how Schoolmaster Barrows' rod felt on my knuckles. I was definitely not his favorite student." Patience joined in his laughter.

"It's really all in the way something is taught," she began seriously. "Why, Schoolmaster Allen constantly asks our opinions about the causes of things, instead of just—"

"Did you say Allen?" he interrupted.

"Yes, William Allen is his name. Do you know him?"

"Perhaps," he answered hesitantly. "Only slightly," he amended.

Thinking that he was not sure if he knew the teacher, she tried to describe him. "Well, he's tall, but not too tall, slim, with dark hair. He is quiet and very intelligent, with interesting ideas. He flatters me by paying attention to my opinions."

"Mmm, yes," he murmured, but seemed ill at ease and suddenly changed the subject. "This Boston summer certainly seems warmer than what we are accustomed to in Plimouth. Don't you think so?"

Her heart sank. He was talking about the weather. She must have misunderstood his interest—only new acquaintances or those forced to speak with the elderly talked of the weather.

"Yes," she answered disappointedly, "perhaps the large number of buildings prevents the ocean breeze from cooling off the town."

The faltering conversation was saved by the arrival of Lily with the ribbon purchase. Patience decided to take pity on Thomas. "There you are Lily. We'd better start back to the house. They'll be wondering what happened to us." She smiled casually at Thomas. "It was nice seeing you again."

"You too." He hesitated. "May I call on you sometime?"

"Oh, yes. That would be fine," she answered before he could change his mind. "Anytime." He waved and hurried on his way down Park Street.

Patience and Lily started back to the Wentworth house. Patience was unnaturally quiet, reviewing the conversation in detail. His initial interest had seemed to disappear so quickly, yet he had said that he wished to see her again. Sighing, she resigned herself to waiting until he called.

Lily trudged along beside her, also absorbed in her own thoughts. She had seen the same quiet look in Anne's eyes, just after her first meeting with Oliver. And look what had happened to Anne after that. Her mistress, no, her friend, had spent the last six months in the throes of high excitement or bitter disappointment. Even jealousy had reared its ugly head. At first, the romance had been truly exciting - the secret exchange of notes, the thrill of not being discovered . . . and she had been such an important part of it all. But now Master Wentworth was so angry when Oliver was nearby. And Anne being trapped in her room like that was so unfair. Was love always like this? Would the same thing happen to Patience? Lily fervently hoped not. Because if this was love, what would happen when it was her turn?

# Chapter 6

That evening Patience dragged the heavy, but only completely comfortable chair in Anne's room, close to the oversized bed. Tucking her feet up under her skirt and trying to act as disinterested as possible, she started to tell Anne about meeting Thomas. "I ran into a friend from home today, Thomas Warren. He mentioned something about calling on us."

"Thomas Warren. I've heard that name before. Isn't he the one who delivered your letter last summer? Interesting. Just how good a friend is he?"

"Well, I've actually known him all my life, although I've seen little of him since he left for Harvard. In the past he was really more a friend of Prudence and Charity." She attempted a slight shrug to underline her indifference, but without much success.

"Perhaps now he'd like to be a friend of yours as well," Anne said, a glint of anticipation in her eye. Then she pointedly asked, "Do you like him?"

Patience tried not to appear to take the question seriously. It would never do to have even Anne guess she may be interested before she knew if Thomas would really call. It would be too embarrassing to be seen as waiting anxiously for him to notice her. So, making a deliberate effort to keep her tone even, she answered as neutrally as possible.

"He's nice enough. It might be pleasant to see someone from home every now and then."

Anne clapped her hands together and happily contemplated the possibilities, "Oh Patience, he sounds perfect. I hope that he calls upon you soon." She continued excitedly, "Wouldn't it be wonderful if each of us had someone special? Of course, it would take time for you to have as deep a friendship with Thomas as I have with Oliver. You would need to know each other much better."

"But Anne," Patience began to protest, "he's just a family friend." Then she inadvertently frowned, instantly reminded of what she had caught sight of the day before.

Seeing her expression, Anne was anxious. Because of their closeness there was no use pretending. "What's the matter? Were you surprised at how I see Thomas?" She became worried, "Or is it Oliver? You do like him, don't you? I know that you haven't had time to get to know him well, but I promise he is everything that is fine and upstanding. I want so much for you to like him, for my sake." She looked imploringly at Patience, who could no longer avoid telling her what she had seen.

Patience took a steadying breath and, meticulously brushing an imaginary crumb from her lap so that she would not be forced to look directly at Anne, began hesitantly, "I'm just worried. When I came upstairs yesterday to tell Oliver that the Balfour carriage could give him a ride home, you didn't hear my first knock on the door . . ."

Anne realized immediately what had happened and coloring slightly, she leaned closer to Patience. "Oh, I see." She kept her voice low to avoid being overheard. "You know we're in love." She added defensively, "We steal moments of affection where we can."

Patience's words tumbled out in a rush of relief that the subject was now in the open, "But do you think that's wise? You're not engaged. And your parents act as if they would like Oliver to simply disappear. It's certain that they would not now bless such a friendship, even if you were to be open about it. You know that what you did is not proper. What if it had been your mother who had come upstairs?"

Anne was indignant, "Proper? Proper? How can you talk that way when Oliver and I love each other so deeply! You are too much a minister's daughter!"

Patience could feel her temper rise instantly. A flush crept up her cheeks. Too much a minister's daughter, indeed! No one had ever accused her of that before. If anything, in the past, others said she did not behave enough like a minister's child. A quick retort was on the tip of her tongue, but with tremendous effort, she bit it back. Her best friend was in serious trouble. What if she and Oliver had been caught? Anne had always been extremely close to her parents and adored by them both. Now she was obviously torn between doing what they wanted and following her own heart, not a choice to be envied. Patience unclenched her teeth, gritted from the unaccustomed effort of holding her tongue, and for once, thought before she spoke. Perhaps she had sounded too prudish.

Meanwhile Anne twisted her fingers nervously and was first to apologize, "Oh Patience, please forgive my quick tongue. It sometimes runs away with me. It's just that I truly need you to be on my side right now. I just have to believe that everything will work out. It simply must!"

Patience was immediately sorry that she had said so much. She had certainly been told often enough that blurting out every thought was one of her worst faults. "I know you're worried and I'm sure everything will turn out fine, but you haven't known Oliver so very long. He may be perfectly nice but—" Her voice lacked conviction. "Just promise me you'll be careful." Although the girls continued to chat further that evening about many small things, the sharp words they had spoken continued to hang in the air.

The next morning Patience got up late, as tired as if she had never gone to bed at all. The mirror was an unfriendly reminder of a night spent tossing and turning. Studying the smudges under her eyes, she spoke sternly to herself. Worrying would help no one. Either the Wentworths would eventually allow Oliver and Anne to become engaged, or the move to Scituate would end the friendship. Her own fretting could not affect either outcome; she just wished she had not seen Oliver threaten that poor boy. He had been so mean. What if Anne's father was right about him?

Soon thereafter, more awake after a hot cup of tea with extra honey, she went to Anne's room to wait for Schoolmaster Allen. Both girls tried hard to put the awkwardness of the past evening behind them, laughing and talking about everything. Everything, except Oliver, of course.

During the morning lesson the tutor concentrated on arithmetic and the girls struggled to understand the problems that he put before them. Once again Patience saw how different teachers could be. At home Schoolmaster Barrows was of the opinion that young ladies needed to know only the most elementary mathematics. Apparently Master Allen did not agree. The problems that he gave were well beyond anything Patience had seen before, and he seemed to feel that his pupils should be able to solve them all.

Often confronted by two blank stares, the tutor carefully explained the answers to the problems.

"Why must we know this?" Anne grumbled. "I will have no need for such complicated figuring!"

"Much of the world's logic is based upon number concepts. It is important for young women, as well as young men, to understand as much logic as possible. After all, it is the women who raise the next generation and must train them early to manage well."

He smiled gently and Patience smiled back. How strange for someone to be concerned about schooling for girls. Then a stray thought popped into her head. How often had Father sat at the kitchen table, helping with her lessons, trying to make her understand what Schoolmaster Barrows had been saying so poorly that day? She thought back. Too many times she remembered, she had been only interested in finishing the work as quickly as possible so that she could move on to something more interesting. Now she really looked forward to hearing about new ideas. How strange. Wouldn't Father be surprised.

That morning Lily did not knock on the door as usual to announce the end of the lesson. Instead, Anne began to fidget when the tutor carried on beyond the normal time, causing him to finally check his pocket watch.

"It looks as though it's time to end for today," he remarked, gathering up his books and papers. Patience bent down to help him find the quills that had rolled away and dropped onto the carpet and, once he had dutifully packed them away in his bag, walked with him down the wide staircase. They met Mistress Wentworth at the bottom of the steps.

"Thank you very much for the lesson, Master Allen," Anne's mother said formally, offering her hand.

Turning to Patience she added distractedly, "I am sorry, my dear, but it appears that Lily has left to do the errands without you. I can't imagine why she didn't wait. I will speak to her about this when she returns."

Patience was sharply disappointed. Because of the continuing unrest in the city, reported in lurid detail in the Boston Gazette, she was not allowed to walk alone and there was no one else free in this busy household. She had become used to her walks with Lily and the house seemed stifling just now. But she would have to wait until the next day to go out.

Master Allen glanced at her unhappy expression.

"Madame, I must visit Wheelers' Stationers near the Mall for new pen nibs. I would be delighted to have Patience come along with me. It will only take a short time. Naturally I will escort her home afterward."

"How kind of you, sir. I know how much Patience enjoys the out of doors. Even our hot Boston August has not discouraged her from her walks. I often admire her energy in this oppressive weather." Having reminded herself of the steamy humidity, she daintily patted her brow with a lace handkerchief. Patience ran up the stairs to her room for a sunbonnet before the schoolmaster could change his mind. She stopped in to tell Anne where she was going.

"A walk with Master Allen?" Anne said, eyebrow arched slightly and feigning a Suzanna accent. "How very interesting," she giggled.

Struggling to tie her hat and not keep the schoolmaster waiting, Patience did not have time to think of a suitably clever reply, and simply mumbled, "Mmm, yes, well. Good-bye," to an amused Anne. She rushed toward the front door.

Once Patience and the young teacher were on their way, comfortably matching strides, she said, "Thank you very much for inviting me along, sir. I do so enjoy being in the fresh air and Anne's parents won't let me walk alone in the city."

"It's my pleasure, Patience. I am sure that they're only concerned because there's so much trouble on the streets at present." He gave her a sidelong glance, "Now that we are beyond the classroom, would you feel comfortable calling me William?"

Pleased to be asked, and suddenly feeling much older, Patience tried out his first name, "It was not my intent to sound as though I were unhappy with the precautions that the Wentworths are taking, William. I'm sure that they have only my safety in mind. Daily life seems so much more . . ." she searched for the word, "anxious here."

"Anxious? What an unusual choice of words. Is life really so serene in Plimouth?"

She thought about his question for a minute, and then replied slowly. "It would seem so. The only event of importance there is my sister Prudence's wedding in January. Of course," she added, thinking a bit about the letters from home, "now my younger brother is eager to join the town militia and my parents are unsure where that will lead. But, on the whole, there doesn't seem to be the same constant political arguments there as here in Boston. Of course, I haven't been home in months. Perhaps it is different now."

"And you've seen such arguments here?"

"As a matter of fact, I've seen two or three very nasty arguments—almost fights—between those who support the British policies and who don't." She paused and thought further, "It is true, of course, that Plimouth does not have shiploads of tea on the way to its wharfside. Perhaps that is the difference."

She instantly remembered the latest trouble she and Lily had seen. "Why, the last time we were out, Lily and I saw a boy shoved and bullied simply for speaking up about those shipments. Someone who works for the governor came and he threatened the boy with jail just for giving his opinion." Patience deliberately didn't mention Oliver by name. His involvement with Anne was difficult enough without making it worse.

William's face clouded as he listened. His shy smile was gone and he spoke with intensity. "Many here in Boston are worried about our troubles with the British. As a tutor I work with a number of young students and most seem to feel that King

George and Parliament interfere too much in colonial affairs. They believe that if we are to be governed by the King's policies, we should have our own representatives in Parliament."

William spoke as he did in the classroom, offering the opinions of others, rather than his own. Patience wanted to ask directly about what he personally thought, but was afraid that such a question might seem impertinent. She held her tongue. She was beginning to think that the British involved themselves too much in colonial matters. Why did they have to control everything? Had it really been necessary to manipulate the price of tea on behalf of that English company? She felt that he might agree with her, but was hesitant to ask.

He interrupted her thoughts. "Ah, we have arrived at the stationers. Come, I will introduce you to Master Wheeler, the finest stationer in all of Boston." He firmly guided her up the steps and through the doors of the large and bustling shop.

A portly older man with a white beard and mustache waved from behind a counter piled high with boxes, and then bustled over to them immediately. She chuckled to herself; he looked exactly like the Dutch Saint Nicholas she had seen in pictures.

Introductions were made and the pen nibs purchased with dispatch, "Saint Nicholas" was charming, proudly showing her his store of supplies, while William stepped into the rear room of the shop for several minutes "to review some new books." William came back with a package tucked securely under his arm. "I could not resist the new geography manual from England."

Master Wheeler exchanged a glance with him. "Yes, I understand it contains some interesting material." He turned to Patience. "You must promise to visit again soon, Miss."

She smiled a bit self-consciously at the attention. "I can see that this will easily become one of my favorite stops."

During their walk back to the Wentworths, William did not mention the British again. She learned that he had been educated at Yale and had come to Boston to teach at the urging of a family friend, Master Quincy, one of the important shipbuilders in the area. She had heard Master Wentworth speak of Master Quincy. Perhaps he had been the one to arrange for William's tutoring. It was clear William felt that he was following a calling, much like a minister. "He certainly is different than Schoolmaster Barrows," Patience thought to herself. The Plimouth schoolmaster was always critical of his students, puffing himself up like a toad to be more important than he really was.

William saw Patience to the Wentworth's entrance. At the bottom of the steps she turned to him. "If it would not be too forward of me to ask, I would enjoy borrowing your new book, after you have read it, of course."

He suddenly looked flustered. "Yes, yes, certainly."

He cleared his throat as she traipsed up the steps under his watchful eye, and added that he was in the habit of walking after lessons and would be delighted to have her company.

She turned back to him quickly. "Oh," she said, without considering whether the invitation had been merely a casual politeness, "if it wouldn't be too much trouble, William, I would enjoy that." He smiled. As he walked away, she thought about how intriguing he was. He spoke with her as an equal, definitely a new experience. During the short walk "William" had replaced "Schoolmaster Allen," but, as she reminded herself firmly, she would have to remember that he was the schoolmaster within the Wentworth household.

She stepped through the opened door, humming to herself as she removed her bonnet and fluffed her hair. Mistress Wentworth was waiting near the entrance hall. As promised, her friend Mistress Tremblay had called upon Amanda Case Canfield. "The elderly Mistress Canfield now resides with her daughter, who is married to a Boston attorney, William Dudley, Esquire," she began slowly. "As it turns out, Master Dudley is a long time acquaintance of my husband. The Dudleys are looking forward to meeting you, Patience. Apparently Mistress Canfield has not shown such an interest in anyone in years. We've all been invited to supper three Saturdays next. Of course, Anne will be unable to go, and is quite disappointed, but Lily will be here to stay with her." Excited about meeting Mistress Dunham's friend at last, Patience threw her arms around Mistress Wentworth's waist, hugging her spontaneously.

Lying in bed that night, after prayers and before finally shutting her eyes for the day, she thought about everything that had happened. She still could not completely forget the argument with Anne. She could tell that Anne remembered it too. She was worried about Oliver. She wished that she understood him better. But she knew that now she must be careful not to be openly critical of the British, lest Anne feel her untrustworthy and stop confiding in her. She blamed herself for blurting out what she had seen. There must have been a better way to let Anne know. "Please, God, help me develop tactfulness, quickly," she prayed.

Then her thoughts turned to William Allen. He was certainly interesting, much deeper and more intense than she had believed at the beginning, and even more handsome. She certainly hoped to walk out often with him. She had the feeling that there was much about which they would agree.

Her last conscious thought was of Thomas Warren. Would he call upon her? She definitely hoped so!

# Chapter 7

Refolding the Boston Gazette along its original crisp edges, Patience sighed, then dropped the paper back in its expected place by Master Wentworth's chair. She gave a rueful laugh, "Minister's daughter, indeed!" In private moments, Anne's comment still rankled even two weeks after the fact, with apologies given and accepted, and pains taken on both sides to avoid certain topics. News in her Plimouth "minister's" house was openly talked about. There she would not have had to read the Gazette in secret.

Master Wentworth had made his displeasure known the first time he had seen her reading the paper. She, oblivious during those early days to what was going on in the world, had not even understood what she was reading. But he had been obstinate about the propriety of the situation. "Completely inappropriate for the eyes of a young lady," he had said. Both Anne and her mother had been puzzled and somewhat shocked that she wanted to read such a political publication. Patience had been equally shocked that they had felt that way. Things were so different at home. She had never taken well to being corrected, and Master Wentworth's disapproval was particularly hard to accept because it seemed so unfair. But, she had reasoned, he hadn't specifically forbidden her reading of the Gazette and therefore she continued to do so, only not where others would see. Of course, availability of news had been one thing, interest another entirely. She knew that she had not been actively involved in talk about politics or town meetings at home because then, much to her father's exasperation, life beyond her own door had seemed irrelevant. Boston certainly was a world away from Plimouth, and so was she.

She sighed again as she thought about the editorial she had just read. In writing about the hated Tea Act, with its tax on goods, Master Edes, one of the Gazette publishers, strongly predicted trouble when the Dartmouth, the first tea ship, reached Boston. The only solution he saw was for the Boston merchants who had been appointed by the King to receive the tea, to refuse to take delivery. If these consignees refused as they had already done in New York, Philadelphia, and Charleston, the tea ships would have to sail back to England with their cargo and trouble could be avoided. But Edes had written that such a solution was unlikely since two of the Governor's sons were numbered among the Boston consignees. Patience thought about that. No, not when there was money to be made, she decided, with a sarcasm that was not in her three months ago. She worried about the publisher's prediction and what kind of trouble there would be. Although the Boston Massacre had happened three years before, people in the city remembered well everything about that snowball fight, especially the five young men who had been killed. The acquittal of that Captain Preston, who they said had been responsible, was still fresh in the minds of many. Musket balls for snowballs everyone had said. Would it come to that again? She took a deep breath, dreading even the thought, and forced herself to consider the possibility. She feared that organized colonial resistance to the latest tea business was inevitable, and then, retaliation from England. What would that mean? She could not even imagine. She tried to think of a way around such a clash. She could not. Perhaps, perhaps if they were lucky, with prayers, such could be avoided. She shuddered involuntarily. She had to talk to William about that on their next walk.

The following day's tutoring lesson was a chore, especially for Anne. Having been assigned to write an essay, she struggled, hampered by the pulleys holding her leg. After the third blot, she threw her quill down in disgust. "Really, what is the purpose of reading all these Englishmen's opinions of taxes I'd like to know? And as for writing our opinions of their opinions, it's utter nonsense."

"Sharing ideas in writing is a way to get to know how others think when we can't meet face to face," William said quietly.

Patience, who was having her own problems conforming to the fine penmanship displayed at Mr. Wheeler's, paused. Obviously he believed that substance, not appearance, was what was important. And thank goodness for that, she thought, with an inward chuckle that unfortunately escaped. Two heads swiveled in her direction at the sound. She coughed quickly to cover her laugh. "Perhaps we should end today's lesson here," William said diplomatically, his eyes twinkling. "Although the calendar notes September, the recent rain has made it warm enough to make a quill slippery to hold." Anne flushed as she looked at her inkblot, then she smiled wryly.

Patience glanced at him, a question in her eyes, and receiving the expected nod in return, hurried to let Mistress Wentworth know that she would be taking her usual walk with Master Allen. She gave an unselfconscious little skip on her way back to join the tutor in the front hall.

Once out of the house, they strolled the length of the first block in easy silence. "What did you think of the Gazette editorial?" he asked, aware of her habit of "borrowing" Master Wentworth's paper. She smiled briefly in a conspiratorial way, but then said seriously, "I can't help but think that the trouble the editor predicted when the tea comes will be a fact." She nodded firmly for emphasis.

"Unfortunately, I think you are right," he said, taking her arm as they crossed a muddy path.

"Do you think that people will simply not buy the tea? Surely the East India Company will not continue to send what they can't sell."

"That would certainly be one solution. But such passive resistance will not satisfy all patriots. Some, I believe, will want a bolder stand."

"Oh, but the patriots must have reasonable leaders. I mean," she paused, thinking of her young brother Sam newly joined in the Plimouth militia, "no one wants violence."

He stopped. There was no one nearby as he turned her toward him and lifted her chin so that their eyes met. "No one wants violence," he agreed soberly, "but sometimes it becomes the only option, despite what one wants." He squeezed her shoulders gently and said with unusual gravity, "Patience, please consider going back to Plimouth soon." He continued to look at her for a long moment, and then turned her back toward the walkway, taking her arm in a firm grip. They continued across the muddy street to Master Wheeler's shop. She was silent, considering not only what he said, but also what he might mean.

"Well, well, my two favorite customers." Master Wheeler beamed as he greeted them. Seemingly oblivious to their serious faces, he began to recount an amusing episode with an earlier customer. Almost before Patience was aware, he had involved her in looking at some new ladies' stationery while William again disappeared into the back room "to peruse some selections."

She was mildly irritated. She, too, would like the chance to look at new books and William always seemed to leave her behind. She started to edge past the stationer, intent this time on reaching the back of the store, but William suddenly reappeared, a paper-wrapped package tucked under his arm. She was further irritated that she had not been quite quick enough to see who belonged to the hand she had briefly glimpsed in the back doorway, the one patting William's shoulder.

Meanwhile, Master Wheeler pressed several sheets of the colored stationery into her hand. "It would truly be a favor to me, Miss Patience, if you would try out this new stock, just to see if the surface is smooth enough." Embarrassed at her unaccountable irritation, she tried to thank him for the gift, but the bookseller merely waved them on their way.

"Master Wheeler is too generous," she explained earnestly to William as they stopped momentarily at the bottom of the steps in front of the shop. "I would have been glad to buy the stationery. It's delightful and I will certainly need more."

"Please don't take away his pleasure," he responded with a grin. "He has already told me that he has a soft spot for pretty young ladies who have been blessed with brains." Giving one of her curls a gentle tug as he fingered its softness, he added, "Especially those who happen to have lovely red hair." She suddenly felt warm all over and opened her mouth to say something, anything, not at all sure what words would come out. Just as suddenly, her jaw dropped. Out of the corner of her eye, she saw Oliver rounding the nearest street corner, coming toward them in the pathway, the elegant Suzanna on his arm. They made a striking couple, both tall, beautifully dressed, and full of the self-confidence that comes with a wealthy birth. Eyeing the scene before her, Suzanna raised one all too well shaped eyebrow. William caught Suzanna's gaze and slowly released Patience's curl, as he stepped protectively closer to her side.

"Hello Patience. And who is this gentleman?" Suzanna said in one breath, looking William up and down appraisingly. Patience had the fleeting, but nonetheless clear impression, that Suzanna couldn't imagine there existed in Boston a young man with whom she was unacquainted.

"Hello, Suzanna, Oliver," Patience replied calmly, but with a clipped tone. "May I present William Allen?" She did not bother with Suzanna and Oliver's last names, an omission for which her mother would have chided her.

"Oh, the tutor," Oliver said, extending his hand toward William, but glancing at Patience's set face. They shook hands hastily. Suzanna echoed thoughtfully, "A tutor? You need a tutor?" Her smile was not a pleasant one.

Oliver interjected quickly, "Actually, the tutoring is mostly for Anne, to keep her busy, you know, while she's in bed."

William looked at Suzanna with a most unimpressed expression on his face. "As a matter of fact, Patience could be a teacher herself if she wished, such is the knowledge she has."

"How interesting." Suzanna's tone, bordering on insulting, reflected that to her it was anything but. Aware that she had not made a conquest of William, she patted her perfectly arranged hair for effect, calling attention to the elaborate curls, and tugged on Oliver's arm. "Come Oliver, or we shall be late for the appointment."

Oliver looked at Patience, whose face mirrored the conflicting emotions she was unable to hide. "Yes, yes, you may be right. Patience, please give Anne my best and tell her I shall be in touch soon." Was there a note of pleading in his voice? He walked away, Suzanna clinging to him possessively.

William touched Patience's arm. "I can see that singularly unpleasant young lady has upset you. I'm sorry if I embarrassed you."

"Embarrassed? Why should you think you embarrassed me?" She was completely bewildered.

"Well, I uh . . ." he nodded at the errant curl still dangling on her cheek.

"Oh William, please don't misunderstand," she responded, waving her hand dismissively. "Suzanna's comments don't bother me in the least. That's just her way. I'm worried because Oliver is a special friend of Anne's and seeing him accompanying Suzanna to an appointment is—well . . ." Unable to come up with a suitable word, she shrugged and began to walk.

"But he's from England," William said automatically, then added almost to himself, "that explains some things." Falling in step with her, he was silent for a moment, "But don't you think there may be more than one explanation for what we saw? Perhaps you shouldn't mention it to Anne until you're sure what it means."

She smiled up at him. "That's precisely the conclusion I've also reached." She added decisively, "I shall say nothing to upset Anne needlessly until Oliver can explain. Goodness knows, they have enough difficulties without my meddling."

"Oh Patience," he laughed, "beautiful and bright. You are unusual." She felt her cheeks grow hot again and, with nothing to say, sped up her pace.

"How did Anne and Oliver meet?" he asked.

Relieved that the topic had changed, she responded slowly, "At a tea at Governor Hutchinson's. Oliver's family are the Mansfields. You may have heard of his father, Lord Mansfield. I believe he's a prominent member of the House of Lords." William nodded, waiting for her to continue. "Oliver is an executive aide to the governor, very close actually."

Rapidly approaching the Wentworths' front steps, she touched his arm lightly. "Please William, don't mention what I've said about Anne and Oliver to anyone. No one knows their friendship is anything special. Perhaps I should have been more discreet, but I think of you as a friend and . . ." She did not finish, but looked at him imploringly.

"Of course, Patience." He reached for her hand still resting on his arm and took it in both of his. "I am your friend. Of course I'll keep Anne's secret." He released her quickly when Henry opened the front door, then tipped his hat, and strode thoughtfully away.

"Miss Anne is entertaining Miss Pamela," Henry offered, stepping back to allow Patience to pass. His tone suggested that he did not approve of Miss Pamela. She headed toward the bedchamber.

Approaching the door, she could overhear Pamela saying archly, "They made such a handsome looking couple." She hurried inside.

"Hello Pamela, what a lovely dress. And weren't you thoughtful to visit so early in the afternoon." Eyeing Anne's pale face, she spoke quickly, intent on distracting Pamela, "But the doctor insists that Anne rest every day at this time in order to regain her strength, I'm sure you understand."

"Of course," Pamela agreed, with a knowing look. She had, after all, accomplished what she had set out to do. "I'll just see myself out." She swished her skirt authoritatively as she exited.

"Oh Patience, that awful girl. I can't believe I used to call her a friend. She couldn't wait to come over to tell me she had a long chat with Oliver and Suzanna over near the Mall." Her voice faltered. "They were out walking together."

"Anne, things aren't always what they first appear. You know that," Patience soothed.

"Perhaps, but even if Oliver is behaving honorably, Suzanna is not. She set her cap for him a long time ago with her parents' blessing. Their business in England has suffered these past few years and Lord Mansfield's wealth is well known. A match between Oliver and Suzanna would make the Balfours extremely happy." She stared bitterly, first at her leg, then at the far wall. "And she's able to walk around, while I am stuck here."

Patience had never seen Anne so desolate, not even when she had first come. She seized her hand. "Doctor Cobb has been so encouraging. I'm sure that it will be just a short time before you are up and about, trying on dresses and going with us to dances where you can see Oliver much more often. Your parents—" Here she hesitated, then ended with conviction, "well, they're bound to see the quality man Oliver is. Why in time—"

"Time is what I don't have," Anne retorted wearily, turning back to Patience. "All too soon we'll be living in Scituate, far away from Oliver . . . and Suzanna." Her face tensed in an effort not to cry. "Oh, I'm so miserable. I wouldn't blame you if you packed your bags and ran all the way back to Plimouth." A tear ran slowly down her cheek as she turned her face back toward the wall, closing her eyes in an effort to shut out the world.

Patience patted her shoulder and whispered, "I'll just leave you for awhile. I'm sure you'll feel much better when you've a chance to rest." She tiptoed away. As she walked down the hall, it struck her that it was the second time someone had mentioned an early return to Plimouth. Perhaps she should give the idea some thought. She went into her room, sat in the straight-backed chair near the window, and attempted to learn some history.

Before she realized, most of the afternoon had passed and she had still accomplished very little in the way of studying, though much more in the way of staring at the back gardens. Looking up, she saw Lily pass by her partially opened door on the way to Anne's room. She thought about calling out to suggest that she leave Anne alone for a time, but caught herself when she saw that Lily was carrying a small folded paper. She waited some minutes, and then slid off her bed and walked down the hall, encouraged by a lilting note she heard in Anne's voice. Anne spied Patience by the doorway.

"Patience," she called, waving her in as Lily slipped out. "I hope you haven't packed those bags yet, though I wouldn't blame you if you had." She laughed. "I was really feeling sorry for myself.

"I'm glad to see you're feeling better. I was worried." Patience sat on the edge of the bed.

"I knew there must be a good reason for Oliver to be with Suzanna," Anne continued bubbling. "It seems that he was more or less forced to escort her when the subject come up during a visit of the Balfours to Governor Hutchinson." She raised her voice to a high falsetto, mimicking Mistress Balfour's piercing tone. "Mistress Balfour was *sooo* afraid Suzanna wouldn't be properly protected in this dreadful town." She continued, speaking in her normal voice. "The appointment was one of Suzanna's. Oliver left her at the door and hurried home to write me all about it." She paused for a breath, "I'm sorry, Patience, to have been so depressed earlier. I hope you won't take my words to heart. I don't know what I would do without you."

"Of course I'll stay but are you sure that everything is—"

Anne eagerly interrupted her, relief evident in her voice. "Everything is fine now that the mystery of Suzanna and Oliver is solved. I know Oliver loves me as I love him. Everything will work out; it has to."

# Chapter 8

A week went by, and with it seven days filled with lessons and walks and few uncomfortable moments. After the crisis over Suzanna had been averted, Patience had been convinced that Anne would begin to talk freely again about Oliver, and so she had purposely mentioned him at breakfast the next morning. But Anne had other ideas. "I feel that you're still unsure about Oliver, Patience, so I've been thinking." She had smiled ever so slightly. "You're my dearest friend and I don't want anything to ruin that friendship. Under the circumstances, I believe that it would be best for us not to speak of him."

Patience had opened her mouth to protest, but had realized almost immediately that she had nothing to say. Her own tactlessness was the reason that Anne would not talk to her now. It was her own fault. She vowed to be more understanding; she would have to break down the barrier between them a little at a time. She must learn to accept Oliver for what he was to Anne, the love of her life.

♦ ♦ ♦

The time for meeting Amanda Case Canfield, Mistress Dunham's childhood friend, had finally arrived. Patience gazed hopefully in the mirror, then smiled. She could not help but be pleased by her reflection. She knew she was being prideful, as her father would say, but pretended it was not so. She twisted slightly to the left, then to the right. She must have grown some since Mother had sewn the elegant green silk dress months before, because now each nip and tuck hugged her figure closely for a rather stunning result, if she did think so herself. Martha, having taken a personal interest in her gradually improving appearance, had curled and ribboned her hair again, brushing furiously until the auburn waves shown with light. As Patience patted the trailing ribbons carefully, she tried to imagine doing the same at home. She shook her head immediately, knowing without a doubt that, even with Jenny's help, she would be unsuccessful. Maybe she could ask Charity. Then she smiled wryly. There were few places in Plimouth where she would need such elegance.

She continued to stare, now unseeing, into the glass, letting her mind wander to thoughts of home and family and her own place as a small town minister's daughter. Not that she would mind going back to the comfort of Plimouth, for even the excitement of Boston could not completely lessen her feelings of homesickness. When she did return, though, she would know that, inside, she was not the same person who had left Plimouth only a short while before. She felt the changes within, not as openly noticeable as the changes in her appearance perhaps, but there nonetheless. She thought of William and a pleasant shiver ran down her spine.

How many of the changes were because of him? Thomas Warren had not called upon her at all. She had waited impatiently for a note or a visit, but by the end of the second week after they had met on the street, she knew that he would not come. She had barely noticed, she told herself, because William had proved to be so fascinating. Teacher and pupil, now good friends, had walked almost every afternoon for the past three weeks, providing a welcome relief from the tension that continued in the Wentworth household. With William she did not need to watch everything she said and did, as she felt she now had to with Anne. Anne had become increasingly irritable about the subject of the King's rights. Patience, trying hard to follow her own advice not to be so opinionated, now bit her tongue before offering even the most offhand comment about the growing unrest over the English presence in Boston. Avoiding the topic of the English and the tea tax was becoming definitely awkward; avoiding the subject of Oliver even more so. Anne remained determined not to talk about him, making Patience very uneasy.

All the servants except Lily had been given the night off. When the carriage left for the Dudley's, Lily and Anne would be alone. At first Patience had been merely sorry that Anne would miss the dinner, but now, thinking further about everything, she was worried. For the past several days, Lily had been going on a ridiculous number of errands for Anne, implying to anyone who asked, that Patience could not go with her because she was taking a turn around the Mall with the schoolmaster. A family of twelve would not have required that many errands, and Patience strongly suspected that the maid was solely a messenger to Oliver. Twice in the past few days she had spied an edge of white paper protruding from the maid's skirt band. What were they planning? Would Oliver visit while they were all away tonight? As uneasy as she was about him, Patience couldn't believe he was the type to sneak around against Master Wentworth's wishes. But then Anne could be most persuasive when she set her mind to something.

She could feel butterflies in her stomach. She could not stop thinking about what could happen if Anne and Oliver met alone. She wished she could talk to her about him. True, Anne was still warm and friendly in every way. In every way, that was except when it came to the handsome Governor's aide. Patience continued trying to persuade her to talk about him; just last night at dinner, as the two had laughed about how much Anne's leg would be stretched by Doctor Cobb's pulleys, she had attempted again, carefully she thought, to bring the conversation around to him. But Anne had turned the question aside and continued to joke about how silly she would look with one leg longer than the other. Patience again wished that she had not blurted out what she had seen happen between Anne and Oliver. Until then they had always confided all their secrets to each other.

Glancing again at the mirror, she realized with a start that her anxiety was too noticeable. That would never do. The Wentworths might ask why she looked so worried; she had never been good at hiding things. Everyone could always tell when she was lying. She deliberately erased a frown, determined not to betray Anne's secret. After all, she was still her best friend. And besides, it might only be her imagination. It would not be the first time that had happened. She practiced a carefree smile, with only modest success.

Deliberately burying Anne's problems in the far corner of her mind, she reached into the back of the bureau drawer, past the chemises and night dresses, and carefully withdrew the golden locket from its resting place. She unwrapped the silk scarf that protected it, and traced the intricate carving with her finger, one last time. She snapped open the clasp and smiled back at the two young girls captured forever in the painting inside. Then she closed the locket, folding it back into the scarf, and placed the tiny package in her purse. Tonight, after sixty years, the locket would be returned to its owner.

She opened a second drawer and rummaged around for a light shawl. With the sun setting earlier, the evenings often turned cool and Master Wentworth had said that they might walk home from the Dudley's. If so, she would need a wrap to ward off the chill. She folded the woolen cover, which didn't match as well as she would have liked, around her arm, and walked slowly into the hall. Glancing once more at her reflection in the long ornate mirror, she coaxed a straying curl into submission, and then knocked on Anne's door.

"Come in, come in. I want to see how beautiful you look," came the quick reply. With a wide grin and a queenly curtsy, Patience presented herself at the foot of the bed.

"Oh my, your dress is lovely. Your mother is such an marvelous seamstress!"

"Yes," Patience said dryly, "at least my sisters inherited her talent!" Anne laughed.

"I hope you'll like the Dudleys. Master Dudley has been Father's lawyer forever. I heard their daughter Priscilla is about to be engaged."

Patience shifted back and forth nervously. "But no one will be here except you and Lily. I feel I should—"

"Don't be silly," Anne interrupted. "I'm going to bed early. I'm feeling a bit tired."

Patience thought that Anne did not look in the least tired. As a matter of fact, she seemed in the peak of health, flushed cheeks and all. Patience looked pointedly at her. "No one is stopping by to visit then?"

Anne was immediately defensive. "Of course not." Patience was at once ashamed of her thoughts. What was wrong with her? She was becoming like one of those suspicious old women whom she had always disliked. Small wonder that Anne no longer fully trusted her. As she said good night, she told herself firmly that it was unfair to doubt that Anne would spend the night exactly as she had said she would.

Moments later Patience was seated opposite the Wentworths in the carriage. The early autumn evening had turned cool after the warmth of the day; there were some reds and yellows and the promise of a new season in the trees that lined both sides of the thoroughfare. Those few leaves that had already trickled down and lay discarded along the way provided a satisfying crunch beneath the wheels of the carriage.

The coach lumbered to a halt before Mistress Tremblay's home, a small, but precise house on a street of other small, but precise houses. Isaac, at his coachman's best, jumped down from the seat and stood officially by the carriage door. An elderly, white-haired butler slowly opened the front door of the house and, with Mistress Tremblay on his arm, doddered down the steps to the carriage. It took a few minutes for Mistress Tremblay's seating to be arranged to the satisfaction of the butler, who was, it turned out, hard of hearing as well as slow of step. But finally they were on their way, the coach creaking and jolting though the cobblestone side streets of Boston. To save their dresses from the dust arising from traffic, Mistress Wentworth had determined that the interior shades must be drawn, making the trip even stuffier and more uncomfortable than usual. Master Wentworth sat stoically throughout the ride, his mouth set in an exasperated line.

At last Isaac reined the horses up in front of an imposing stone house on fashionable Marlborough Street. The front door opened immediately and a thin man in gray livery and an immaculately powdered wig ran down the steps to grab the reins and tie them securely to the brightly polished post. He helped the ladies from the carriage and, with mincing steps, escorted them inside.

The Dudleys were waiting in the front parlor and introductions were quickly completed. Mistress Canfield was nowhere in sight. As they exchanged pleasantries in the ornate room, with its Louis XIV formal upholstered furniture crammed in every nook and cranny, Mistress Dudley explained her mother's absence.

"Dear Mama is quite frail and often rests. But she is most anxious to visit with all of you and will join us for supper. Please take your ease. Let us enjoy some of Cook's punch before our meal." With great affectation, the downstairs parlor maid began to pour and distribute the drinks.

Mistress Dudley sat next to Patience and took her hand. "My mother is so looking forward to hearing about Mistress Dunham. Why, I have not seen her this interested or alert in years. After Mistress Tremblay called upon her, she told me stories of her childhood with Mistress Dunham, tales that I had never heard before. The revival of these memories is a marvelous tonic for her." Mistress Dunham's charm completely changed Patience's initial impression of a plain woman. Her comfortable way easily explained her reputation as the "simply wonderful hostess" Mistress Tremblay had described.

Patience quickly remembered the manners firmly insisted upon by her mother. "This is a wonderful chance for me to do a good turn for a friend. It's most kind of you to invite me along with the Wentworths."

Out of the corner of her eye, she saw that the men sat to the side in the parlor, absorbed in what appeared to be an increasingly heated discussion about something which, she sensed, they agreed. Their wives took turns shooting pointed glances at them, trying to no avail to draw them into their bland exchange about mutual friends. As curious as ever, Patience tried hard to overhear the conversation. What were they talking about? She thought she caught mention of the word "Adams" and "the Dartmouth." They must be talking about the British. The tea ships were now on their way from England, and their anticipated arrival was the topic of anxious conversation on every street corner. She was unable to overhear anything further without being too obvious. Eavesdropping was one thing; getting caught at it was something else.

Through an open window the murmur of voices drifted in from the garden. Seeing Patience's glance, Mistress Dudley smiled. "Our daughter Priscilla is taking a turn in the garden with my husband's new law clerk. They will be joining us shortly. He is a pleasant young man and often invited to dine with us."

Mistress Tremblay rose to admire a finely crafted silver bowl on the sideboard, "What a wonderful shine the silversmith has created on this piece."

"Yes," Mistress Dudley agreed, walking over to join her at the elaborately curlicued sideboard. "We were so fortunate to find a craftsman of Master Revere's skill here in the city. He has a quite a lovely shop not too far from here, if you'd like me to give you directions."

"Oh, I do believe I've seen his sign. I shall have to stop by on my next outing. I—" She stopped and looked up as two people appeared in the doorway. Patience was stunned when a beautiful young woman entered the room—with Thomas Warren by her side. They stood for a moment framed in the light. She was almost as tall as he, slim and willowy, with shining black hair wound at the nape of her neck and vivid dark eyes. Patience's heart lurched.

"Why, here are Priscilla and Thomas now," Mistress Dudley said.

Mistress Wentworth looked pleased, "What an agreeable surprise to find Thomas Warren here. We have already met. He is a Plimouth friend of the Burgess family. Priscilla, it's lovely to see you again."

Master Wentworth rose from his chair and moved toward the couple. He gallantly kissed the back of Priscilla's hand and shook Thomas' heartily. Mistress Tremblay nodded politely, while Patience tried valiantly to swallow the lump in her throat.

After the introductions, conversations continued, and Thomas walked Priscilla toward the chair where Patience sat, unusually silent. Now Patience understood why he had not called on her. Priscilla was a truly lovely looking and apparently charming young woman, a couple of years older than herself, she guessed. Obviously he was spending time with her instead. Anne had said Priscilla was about to become engaged. Why did it have to be to Thomas? She forced a smile.

"Priscilla, Patience is staying with the Wentworths until the holidays," Thomas explained. "Their daughter, Anne, had an accident last summer, and Patience is keeping her company during her convalescence."

"How kind of you, Patience," Priscilla said. "I'd heard about Anne's fall. It must be very difficult for her to stay out of society for such a long time. I know that I'd certainly be out of sorts."

Even if she had wanted to, Patience would have found it difficult to dislike Priscilla. She was such a friendly person that she found herself warming to her in spite of the inevitable jealousy she felt. It certainly was not her fault that Thomas had chosen her instead.

Patience tossed her head and tried to keep the flush from her cheeks. "Actually, it's been a very exciting time for me. Anne's friends visit often, and, of course, there are many lessons to do. I am also fortunate indeed to be able to walk daily with my friend, William. He's introduced me to Master Wheeler, who has that large stationery shop off the Mall. Master Wheeler is a most entertaining gentleman, who seems to know all the latest news in Boston. We stop by often just to chat. I am enjoying myself *ever* so much."

Thomas' eyebrows rose when she mentioned William. Even though she was rambling in the same artificially bright voice she detested in Suzanna, she was secretly satisfied that she had been able to let him know in such a casual way that she had not been just sitting in the parlor waiting for him to call.

"Oh, I too enjoy walking. I traipse about nearly every day with Nathaniel Yardley, my fiancé." Priscilla smiled agreeably, "It's so stimulating to be out of doors, especially now that the summer heat has broken."

Nathaniel Yardley? Fiancé? She could not believe it. She had been too hasty in jumping to the wrong conclusion again. It was just that they had looked like such a perfect couple coming into the room. She glanced over at Thomas. If she were not mistaken,

He had seemed unhappy when he heard her mention William. Perhaps it was not too late to fix things.

"Yes, it certainly is. I'm disappointed on the days when it's not convenient for . . . Master Allen . . . to escort me. He has so many other duties and students that I don't like to burden him too much with my company."

"I'm sure it's not a burden," Priscilla began. But her train of thought was lost with the announcement of dinner. Everyone made way to the lavishly set dining table. The wall sconces had been turned up, and the light reflected off the silver and crystal, bathing the room in a pleasantly soft glow. Mistress Dudley guided everyone toward places at the table, and Patience saw that the seat next to hers was empty. But, almost immediately, an elderly lady was escorted into the room. She was very slight and depended heavily on both her silver-headed cane and the footman's arm. Mistress Dudley began the introductions of her mother, Mistress Amanda Case Canfield.

When it was Patience's turn, Mistress Canfield took her hand and smiled warmly, "My dear, I am so pleased to meet a friend of Elizabeth. I did not know that she was still on this earth, let alone back in Plimouth. You must tell me all about her."

Together they walked to their neighboring places at the table. Patience noticed that Thomas had been seated beside the Wentworths and that the three of them had begun to talk.

She settled into her chair and spoke of Mistress Dunham. Heads bent close together, she and Mistress Canfield spent the entire meal catching up on the lives of two childhood friends. Patience told of the death of Mistress Dunham's beloved Silas so many years before, and Mistress Canfield of her marriage, late in life, to Hollings Canfield. Master Canfield had been a wealthy widower when he married Amanda Case and brought her to the very house where they all now lived. Finally, Patience spoke of the locket.

"Oh, I remember it so clearly," the elderly woman said, her candid blue eyes retreating to a faraway place. "My father carried it back from one of his travels. Inside there was a miniature painting of Elizabeth and me. I remember distinctly the day the painting was done. We had gone on a picnic with my father. You see, my mother died when I was born and, as a sea captain, my father was often away. Each time he returned was like my birthday." She smiled, thinking back. "He spoiled me dreadfully. That day it was a picnic that I wanted, and Father took us to the point near the harbor. We spread a quilt on the grass and ate our midday meal; Papa, dressed in his black suit with his dapper mustache carefully waxed, tried hard to keep two highly excited little girls occupied."

Mistress Canfield sighed deeply and laid down her fork as the scene unfolded in her mind. "There was an artist set up nearby with his easel, dabbling at a painting of the harbor. I begged Papa to have a likeness done of Elizabeth and me. He finally asked the artist, explaining to him that I was a most insistent child, and would not leave until I had what I wanted." She shook her head at the memory. "Of course, I had thought that the painting would be of the usual size. But the artist was a clever man who wanted to get back to his business of painting Boston Harbor, and so, in a short time he completed a miniature, satisfying the whim of an indulged child. My father showed me that the locket was a perfect place to keep the little painting. I gave the locket to Elizabeth when she left Boston so that she would remember me. It all was so very long ago, yet I remember it as if it were yesterday."

"Mistress Dunham kept it close to her all these years and always held out the hope that she would be able to give it back to you one day," Patience said. "When she learned that I would be in Boston for a time, she asked me specially to try my best to find you and return the locket." She reached into her pocket, withdrew the jewelry, the symbol of a deep friendship, and held it out. Mistress Canfield reached for the gold pendant, shining in the candlelight.

Talk around the table had stopped and everyone watched them. Patience met Thomas' glance.

"I don't know what to say," Mistress Canfield began, her voice cracking with emotion as she took the locket. Patience swallowed hard, not trusting herself to speak.

Fortunately for them all, at that moment the servants brought in the flaming dessert with great fanfare and dimming of sconces.

The break allowed everyone to clear a throat or wipe a tear without notice.

After every morsel of the delicacy had been consumed, the party retired to the parlor to, as Master Dudley put it, "let our food settle."

Some time later Master Wentworth indicated that they would take their leave, walking the short distance home to take advantage of the lovely night air. Master Dudley understood, "It will be too cold for pleasure walking soon enough." A collective shiver ran through the room at the thought of the Massachusetts winter coming quickly upon them. Thomas indicated that he too would go along with them.

As their wraps were being brought, Patience chanced to be standing near the entry hall, and noticed Master Wentworth and Master Dudley again in deep conversation, this time joined by Thomas.

Her first thought was to retreat, remembering her father's scoldings about her eavesdropping. But, she reasoned to herself, if she did not move closer to deliberately listen, it was not really eavesdropping. She stayed where she was.

She actually overheard very little, but the words that she did catch were confusing. Master Dudley said something about Josh Quincy agreeing to be one of the leaders. Unfortunately, his voice had trailed off at that point in the sentence and Patience did not hear of what he was to be a leader. Was Josh Quincy the same Joshua Quincy who was William's sponsor here in Boston? Master Wentworth said that Sam Adams had also agreed to be involved. That was a name she knew from the stories in the Gazette. Both David and William had talked of him as an outspoken opponent of the tea tax. But why would they be talking about Wheelers' Stationers?

The men shook hands as she took her wrap from the footman. She edged away from the entry just as Thomas turned around. Turning back, she looked directly into his deep blue eyes. They mirrored a quizzical expression. She willed herself not to blush.

They walked away together from the Dudley home, the Wentworths in front escorting Mistress Tremblay. Thomas offered Patience his arm and they followed together a discreet distance behind. She had a difficult time trying to contain her excitement.

"I'm so delighted that I was able to play a part in bringing two such old friends together again. Do you think that Mistress Canfield will write to Mistress Dunham immediately? Should I write to her myself tonight? I would not want her to be startled when she receives a letter from her friend."

As her words rushed on, she realized that Thomas was looking at her with an expression that she could not quite understand. Why did she have to go on so when she was excited! He must find her so extremely young. She must find something else to talk about. "Have you known Priscilla long?"

"Since I came to Harvard. Nathan Yardley was the first friend I made at college, and even then he was in love with Priscilla. It was actually with her help that I was able to obtain my clerkship. I'm very grateful to her. Now that Nathan's study is coming to an end, they're engaged." He was silent a moment, then added, with a slight shrug, "They seem very happy. Perhaps knowing someone well before taking such an important step is wise."

He drew her closer to his side, helping her avoid a puddle in the walkway. She found the closeness exciting, but tried to concentrate on their conversation.

"That could be. Prudence and Jeremiah have been keeping company for two years, ever since he came for further ministry study with Father."

"How are the wedding plans coming? They must miss your help at home."

They paused by Mistress Tremblay's home as the Wentworths delivered her back to the care of her elderly butler. Standing alone with Thomas, Patience wondered if he was teasing her. He must have heard of her lack of skill from her sisters. But she decided to be very cool in her response, "Oh, Mother has all the arrangements made. Other parish women are helping with the necessary handwork. Because my skills in that area are not what they should be, the sewing is probably progressing more swiftly without me." Suddenly she remembered some additional news, "Do you remember Matthew

Potter? From my parents' last letter, it would seem that he's seriously courting Charity."

As they continued on their way, she looked at him out of the corner of her eye. Would Matthew's attention to Charity bother him? Some had thought that he and Charity . . . But Thomas smiled and seemed genuinely pleased that another Burgess match might be on the horizon. "I knew Matthew well at school. I understand he'll be a journeyman shortly and help his father run the family mill at Herring Run." Then he added, teasingly, "Does this mean that you're next in line?"

She was saved from having to answer by their arrival at the Wentworth house and Master Wentworth's hearty statement, "Well, back the same day. Now wasn't that a pleasant walk?"

They all agreed that the brisk outing was just what they had needed after their rich meal. Thomas held Patience's hand briefly, "Since you're without an escort at times, I'd be pleased to walk with you any late afternoon after I've finished my work for Master Dudley." He rushed on without waiting for her reply.

"Would tomorrow afternoon at half past four be convenient for you?"

She smiled, graciously she hoped, "I do happen to be free. I'll see you then."

After a few more pleasantries, he said good night. Patience went up the steps with Mistress Wentworth, who looked approvingly at Thomas, fast disappearing down Salem Street. "It will be so pleasant for you to have a friend from home to keep you company."

Master Wentworth nodded decisively. "Nice young man, ambitious and with an intelligent view of our difficult Boston situation." Patience looked at him closely. Would he prefer someone like Thomas for his daughter?

She went immediately to Anne's room to tell her everything, but when she peeked in, Anne was fast asleep. She was disappointed, but did not wake her. Tomorrow would be soon enough to share the excitement of the evening, an evening that she would remember for a long time.

# Chapter 9

"Well?" Anne asked at breakfast the next morning. "Well," she repeated insistently, "what happened?" The table next to the bed was laden with breads and cheeses and the peach marmalade they were so fond of, most of which was to remain uneaten during the questioning process. Patience began her report, but too slowly for Anne, who kept interrupting. "When did Mistress Canfield say she would write Mistress Dunham? What did Priscilla wear?" and of most urgent interest, "What precisely did Thomas say when he left?" Patience faithfully repeated each conversation as closely as she could remember it twelve hours later, and realized once more how hard it must be to be imprisoned in a room, dependent upon others for scraps of secondhand news. On this crisp September morning, when the trees were tinged with autumn colors and the birds called to one another, Patience would soon crunch through the early leaf fall, inhaling the brisk sea air, as she did every day. Anne would be forced to watch from the window, as she did every day.

Patience reached for the chocolate pot, perched somewhat precariously at the edge of the table, and splashed the hot mixture into the cups. "Has Doctor Cobb decided which day he'll change your leg strapping?"

Anne's face radiated excitement. "Yes, on Tuesday next he and that miserable assistant of his—heaven forgive me, I dislike the man—will come in the morning to replace this contraption with a shorter one, only to my knee this time. And it will not need to be padded with pillows. Doctor Cobb said that finally I will be able to move about and leave this room." She grinned, contemplating the possibilities, "I'll even be able to go outdoors, though not walking alone yet, of course." She added with obvious delight, "Actually, the doctor suggests that I get out as much as I can. He said that I need the fresh air to fully recuperate." Her broad smile extended well beyond its usual limits. "Papa is having the men at the shipyard make me an invalid chair, you know one of those chairs with wheels, and then I'll be able to get around ever so much more easily." She became suddenly pensive, "I am truly grateful that I'm mending at last. Before my fall I had never thought what it would be like to be unable to walk. I have had nothing but empty hours to think, and I know now that I have taken much too much for granted. I've promised myself that I'll never do so again."

Patience clapped her hands eagerly. "How wonderful! We'll have such a splendid time when you're at last able to move around. Will the chair be light enough for me to push?" She decided, "I'll take you everywhere with me!"

"Wait a minute, Patience," Anne shook her head laughingly. "You may well have not one, but two interesting men to walk with," she teased. "We mustn't discourage them with my presence."

Patience blushed at the statement; there did seem to be an unusual abundance of men at the moment. She was on the verge of trying to convince Anne that she really meant the invitation when she suddenly realized that it was more likely that Anne wanted time alone to be with someone else, someone like Oliver Mansfield. Would she now be able to meet him away from the vigilant eyes of her parents? No sooner had that thought popped into her head than Patience chided herself. Anne undoubtedly had the most unselfish of motives for wanting her to have time alone with William and Thomas and here she was, looking for double meanings in everything. What was the matter with her? Lately she was constantly suspicious, even of poor William's wish to look at a book at Wheeler's without her underfoot. She had to stop thinking like this.

Anne continued on, insistently bringing her back to the conversation, "And there'll be something else to celebrate my freedom. A party. For my seventeenth birthday, that is. My parents are inviting everyone Mother can think of, even Father's business friends. As a matter of fact, I think Governor General

Hutchinson and his wife are also being asked." She thought a moment, and then added, not quite in an undertone, "Although lately Father seems even more upset than usual with that man."

Patience offered, "Maybe because the tea everyone's worried about is finally on its way from London."

But Anne simply shrugged and refused to consider her father's business problems. Her happiness could not be diminished in any way. "Who knows? Who cares? It'll really be a marvelous night, just marvelous. I shall invite both Masters Allen and Warren. Then you'll have at least two men competing for your attention." She giggled mischievously, "Who knows, perhaps there will be even more."

Patience automatically protested, "Anne, you know that William is not competing for my attention."

"And what of Thomas?" Anne asked, with a falsely innocent air. The flush on Patience's cheeks answered for her.

♦ ♦ ♦

A few days later Patience saw firsthand what arrangements for the party, already in full advance, involved. She recalled wryly that in Plimouth when there had been an "at home" at the parsonage, she and her sisters had been assigned the tasks of parlor cleaning and baking. Making sure that there were no corner cobwebs and that the teacakes were light enough had been Mother's main concern. It was apparent, however, that in the Wentworth household, "preparation" took on a whole new meaning. Every drapery in the house was removed for washing, extra chairs had been brought in from the carriage house for cleaning, and cases of preserves, wine, and fruits had been released from their dark cellars. Mistress Wentworth's desk in the back parlor resembled a brigade command post from which she issued orders to the servants who presented themselves early each morning. No cushion was to remain uncleaned, no step unscrubbed, no rug unbeaten. Patience stood in awe. She and Anne were delegated to address the invitations and given to understand in no uncertain terms that they should otherwise remain out of the way of the serious work.

As the days went by, however, there was trouble. One evening Master Wentworth had appeared in the downstairs sitting room where Patience and Anne were relaxing. Anne had looked up from the piece of lace she was dutifully trying to embroider. "Papa, Oliver may be a little late to the party. He—" Patience had been startled at the sharp tone in Master Wentworth's voice.

"Daughter, obviously you have not heard what I've been saying. It is bad enough I have to pretend to be friendly to Loyalists we already know. I refuse to add some British stranger to the list. Let me be very clear. Oliver Mansfield is not invited."

Anne's voice had risen angrily, "He's not a stranger, and you've asked the Balfours and others like them! Why not Oliver?"

"That will be enough of that, Anne," Master Wentworth had said in a tone that left no room for further discussion. "They're long time business contacts, and in another category entirely."

No amount of pleading or crying on Anne's part persuaded the Wentworths to change their minds and invite him. At first, she was beside herself and, momentarily forgetting her decision to avoid the subject of Oliver, talked endlessly to Patience about the unfairness of it all. Patience tried to listen sympathetically, but even though she had promised herself that she would make an effort to be friendlier to Oliver, was unable to muster anything beyond, "Oh, Anne, you must be so upset." This response, Anne's expression warned, was completely insufficient. Soon Anne spoke of Oliver less and less, until finally she spoke of him not at all.

♦ ♦ ♦

Time flew. Doctor Cobb, a thin, bird-like man, with little hair and less humor, accompanied by his portly assistant who barked orders at the drop of a hat, arrived on the appointed day to remove the strapping on Anne's leg. Having been assured that there would be little pain in the process, Patience asked to stay with Anne, but with smug superiority, the assistant, Master Marshall, highhandedly denied her request without even consulting the doctor. So Patience, Mistress Wentworth, and Lily hovered together outside the entrance to the bedchamber while one wrapping was substituted for another.

Finally the door was pushed ajar and Anne stood radiantly in the opening, her hand resting heavily on Doctor Cobb's arm for support. There was a moment of silence, and then an exuberant explosion of hugs, shouts, and a few tears of joy.

The doctor waited impatiently until the excited commotion died down before he spoke, pompously as always, "Mistress Wentworth, I am quite pleased with your daughter's recovery. It would appear that the break was not as severe as we had first feared. However, I have told her that it is most important that she follow my instructions precisely." He paused, and added in measured tones, "For if she does, if she does, this last wrapping may be removed before Christmas and her leg will be as good as new." He cleared his throat to emphasize the importance of his opinion.

Mistress Wentworth held her daughter tightly as she absorbed the doctor's directions. "Will Anne be permitted to move around with her leg wrapped like this? My husband is having his men fashion an invalid chair so that she may be pushed about, if you approve, that is,"

Doctor Cobb nodded sagely, appearing to ponder his answer, then weighed each word. "The covering on your daughter's leg now is for support and to allow the bone to strengthen. She may move slowly within the perimeter of the house and garden, provided that she has someone to help her. The chair is an excellent idea for longer walks. Please understand that she is to be encouraged to be out of doors as much as possible. She is looking quite peaked from her long stay inside the house and we must improve her constitution." Mistress Wentworth's determined expression left no doubt that his instructions would be followed to the letter.

That night the chair was delivered by two of the burly workmen from the shipyard and a jubilant Anne tried it out. Resembling a regular sturdy seat, with strong pieces of wood connecting the legs, it had round wheels attached underneath, allowing the chair to move easily. Everyone in the Wentworth household took turns pushing it around the house to get its feel.

Patience and Anne fell into gales of laughter when Lily was unable to negotiate a sharp turn by the dining table and ended up navigating Anne into a corner facing the wall.

Master Wentworth decreed that the chair should be stationed in the first floor parlor. Each afternoon after lessons, Isaac was to carry Anne downstairs so that she could take a turn in the garden, and then remain "up and around."

◆ ◆ ◆

Within a few days the girls settled into their new routine. Although it was still only Patience who looked forward to the lessons, they were both ready at a moment's notice to sit happily in the back garden. The summer flowers had gone by; there was nothing to be done about that, but Merchant, the fussy gardener, planted more chrysanthemums than usual, knowing that "Miss Anne" would be enjoying their vibrant colors.

Anne continued to insist, however, that Patience go on her daily walks with both William and Thomas, and, because the walks remained Patience's closest link to the outside world, persuasion was easy.

From the start, back weeks and weeks before, the time with William always ended at Master Wheeler's stationery shop. She was beginning to know the crinkle-eyed "Saint Nicholas" very well. She could tell that, over time, he had become comfortable with her too, for he and William now spoke openly about trouble with England, something that many people were reluctant to do. As a matter of truth, most of the time, the men seemed to forget entirely that she was there. At first, Patience had been shocked at how passionately outspoken William was about colonial rights. Away from the Wentworth home, he quickly dropped his deferential manner. His eyes blazed as he held forth, "They must understand that we will not be taxed without a say in the matter. That is all there is to it." He continually added to his list of grievances about England: "They bleed us with taxes to pay for their infernal war; they treat us like prisoners with regiments at Castle William; now they intend to send us that blasted—excuse my language, Patience—tea! How can they, a world away, understand our colonial needs? I say now, as I've said all along, we should either be represented in Parliament or have our own damn—sorry Patience—government!" Lately, he had become even more insistent that an independent government should be formed. At first it had been a frightening thought for Patience, but he spoke as if he were only one of many who believed so. The idea, once planted, soon became more acceptable to her.

In spite of his anger, however, he was always able to curb his tongue in front of Anne. He said nothing in the classroom and changed back each day, seemingly effortlessly, into his role as the mild schoolmaster, gently prodding his students into thinking for themselves. Remembering how she had too often blurted out something without thinking, Patience knew that she could learn much from his self-control.

During the first visits to the shop, Master Wheeler had tried to argue with William about the reasons for England's behavior: "All colonies are governed that way, monies for protection, that's the way it has always been." As the weeks went on, however, his justifications had become half-hearted at best. He no longer defended the King's position as right, but pleaded caution instead, "Be patient, William, please, please. Change comes slowly." As she watched the men, Patience tried in vain to remember if she had ever heard such talk in Plimouth. She was sure she hadn't. But then, she had to admit, she had paid little attention to anything there except extremely insignificant things that had seemed terribly important at the time.

The daily debates forced her to weigh matters for herself. One perfectly ordinary Tuesday morning in mid October, it dawned on her that she no longer accepted England's rule as the way things should always be. She could not pinpoint exactly why she had come to think so. Perhaps it was because of William's constantly critical arguments; perhaps it was because of the highhanded behavior of many British officials; perhaps it was simply because of the heartbreaking stories of those whose survival on the edge of poverty was made so much more difficult by the unfair protection of England's goods. But for whatever reason, she knew that she had changed her mind about how life should be. She did not tell anyone. She needed time to think further about how she felt.

♦ ♦ ♦

Patience also continued to see Thomas. Fortunately, he could only come in the late afternoons, long after William had left, and she had not had to refuse either one of them. The time with Thomas was different, filled with small talk that helped them get to know each other in a way they had not before. As time passed and Patience had caught up with what he was doing at school and at his job, she tried to find out about his political beliefs. Feeling her own sympathies veer toward colonial rights, she was anxious to see if he agreed. At first she was subtle, "I've heard that the Committee of Correspondence has been in touch with men in New York and Philadelphia about the tea deliveries. I understand that they are just as upset as people here about accepting those shipments."

"Mmm, really," was Thomas laconic and quite unsatisfactory response. As tenacious as ever, she became more direct, more obvious. "Do you think that those who insist on more independence for the colonies are treasonous?" But even to that pointed question (which she feared appeared rather rude), he only mumbled something indiscernible and changed the subject. His complete disinterest in what was happening around him was most frustrating. How could he not be interested in the political forces that were swirling about the city? She did not understand.

♦ ♦ ♦

The day of Anne's party dawned crystal clear, with the crisp edge that only a New England October can give. The house was finally in a state of readiness. Even last minute polishing of the ornate silver service in the dining room had been completed. Almost everyone to whom an invitation had been sent had accepted with pleasure. Word was passed that Governor General Hutchinson and his wife were expected.

Patience had overheard the Wentworths discussing their invitation to the Governor's. Master Wentworth had said that because of the tea, feelings were "running high." But he had known that the Governor would be slighted if he were not invited and, wanting to maintain the status quo for the present, had decided that he and his wife should be included. Mistress Wentworth had warned, "Many like Jeremiah Cotton and Bartholomew Foster are violently opposed on this tea business. Those two are no longer even speaking to each other. We must be careful about possible arguments during the party. It wouldn't do to have Anne's evening spoiled by unpleasantness."

Master Wentworth had nodded and added, "An argument between those two would do more than spoil one social occasion. We must be ready to step in at the first sign of trouble."

Over the past few months, Patience had come to realize that Master Wentworth relied heavily on his wife's opinions. At first Patience had assumed that Anne's mother was exactly what she appeared to be: a shy, quiet woman, unknowing in the ways of the world, interested only in keeping her husband and child happy. But she had been misled by the obvious. Why, even Master Wentworth, as strong willed as he was, looked to her for advice. Of course, he did so only when there was no one nearby. She had seen them talking even more often during the past several weeks, Master Wentworth, tall and imposing, his head bent toward his petite wife, listening closely while they walked in the garden each night after supper.

At first she had thought that they must have been talking about Anne and Oliver. But lately, she had come to believe that their concerns were of a different sort entirely. She had caught the drift of words like "Loyalists" and "Parliament" and "that insufferably inept King George." She heard nothing whatever to do with their daughter.

Brushing these thoughts aside, Patience ran up the stairs and rapped rightly on Anne's door.

"Come in, Patience. I know it's you."

"A marvelous birthday to you," Patience said with a grin, as she peeked around the doorjamb. "I can't wait until tonight to give you my present. Would it spoil everything to have it now?"

Anne was dressed in a morning robe of sprigged flowered muslin and sat next to a warming fire, laid early that morning as a testament to the changing temperature. With her color high from the warmth of the flames, and her curls held back, she looked like an exuberant child. "Of course not! Come sit by the window with me. What a glorious day!"

Patience held out the tiny box that she had concealed behind her back, and waited eagerly as Anne removed the slightly messy wrapping and off center ribbon.

"Oh, Patience," Anne gently fingered the silver pin nestled in the box, "how lovely." The tiny oval piece was covered with a hand tooled filigreed design.

"It opens, look, here's the clasp." Patience pointed to the bottom of the pin.

Anne slid her nail between the two halves of the pin and opened it to reveal a place for a picture. She looked over at Patience, "I know. You wanted us to have something like Mistress Canfield's locket to remember our friendship. It's a wonderful idea. I shall wear it always. Wherever did you find it?"

"There's a silversmith nearby, a Master Revere. Deirdre and I visited his shop one day and there it was." She added, "Now we just need an artist to paint us."

"Before you return home, we'll have a painting done," Anne promised. "I'll ask Father. Surely he'll know where we can find someone like that. I shall wear the pin on my gown this evening, everyone will compliment me on it, and I'll tell them that it was a gift from my dearest friend."

The sounds of last minute preparations seeped into the room. Footsteps raced up and down the stairs in constant succession, and Mistress Wentworth's usually delicate, ladylike voice took on a general's tone as she gave final instructions to the servants. Soon she came to give Anne a birthday hug. After finding the perfect place for the pin on Anne's gown, she suggested firmly that the girls rest for the afternoon. Reluctantly, they agreed and after the midday meal, went off to their separate rooms, where even Patience, tired from the excitement of anticipation, slept.

◆ ◆ ◆

Dusk settled upon the Wentworth house, the wall candles were lit, and the household stood at attention waiting for the first arrival. Dressed in the green silk dress Mother had sewn,

Patience felt elegant, somehow beautiful, and a little nervous about meeting so many important people.

It was Anne's first chance to wear her pink dress from Madame Toussignant's shop. She sparkled with excitement. Her creamy skin blended with the richness of the silk, and her dark blue eyes matched the sapphire earrings that she had successfully begged to borrow from her mother.

The Wentworths, both dressed splendidly, positioned themselves in the front hall to receive guests. Patience was struck by their contrast to her own parents. Pastor and Mistress Burgess wore their plain clothes proudly, and she had always been taught that finery was frivolous. She was coming to understand, however, that how one appeared on the outside really had little to do with the kind of person one was on the inside.

At last there came a crunch of wheels on stone, and Isaac sprang from his place on the front steps to open the first of what promised to be a long line of carriages. The lead couple made their way up the steps and handed their collective wraps, gloves, and walking stick to the front door footman, who had been borrowed from the neighbors and pressed into service for the occasion. Henry, in a position of honor, formally announced the arrival, "Master and Mistress Hunter Buckingham," and the guests marched forward, hands outstretched, smiles firmly fixed. Before they completed their greetings, the butler announced others. In less than an hour the house was filled with people, swirling around each other, anxious to be noticed.

"Oh look, here comes William," Patience whispered to Anne. "Your parents are greeting him most warmly. I didn't realize he knew your father so well."

"His sponsor, Master Quincy, is a particular friend of Father's," Anne murmured dismissively, as William inched his way toward their place in the reception line.

"Best wishes on your special day, Anne," he said, a slight smile upon his face.

Anne's correct formal tone matched his exactly, "Thank you for coming, Master Allen." She grinned and added in a tone that carried two couples deep, "If I'm not mistaken, I believe that you've already met Miss Burgess." They laughed, but the push of those in line behind him waiting to be introduced prevented anything more than a few words and a brief handshake.

Finally the crowd of arriving guests moved away from the door, and dispersed into the spotlessly prepared formal rooms. Anne and Patience retreated to a less crowded corner in the front parlor to watch the late arrivals. An insistent older woman had waylaid William, and Thomas had not yet arrived. Patience wondered whether he had forgotten the invitation. She had reminded him just yesterday when they had meandered the length of Tremont Street talking about recently received letters from home. As she was considering the unhappy possibility that he might not come, Isaac announced the arrival of Governor and Mistress Hutchinson. Patience quickly helped Anne back to their places next to the Wentworths. The Governor and his wife swept through the entrance, causing a general murmur among those guests in the vicinity of the hall. Patience had the impression of a dour man, well into middle age, and a plump wife wearing too many jewels. She had heard so much about the Governor that she anxiously awaited her introduction. This would certainly be something to talk about in Plimouth!

She noticed that Anne was smiling broadly and looking at a point directly behind the governor. Why, that point was Oliver! What was he doing here? Then she heard the Governor say to Master Wentworth, "Ah, George, have you made the acquaintance of my aide, Oliver Mansfield? The Earl of Mansfield's son, you know. Great help to me. Rarely go anywhere without him."

Anne's father swallowed hard as he extended his hand to Oliver. "Yes, yes, we've met. I believe that Oliver knows my daughter and many of her friends."

Trying valiantly to mask his displeasure, Master Wentworth completed the greetings quickly, and then, with his wife stroking his arm in a calming way, escorted the Hutchinsons into the parlor, leaving Anne and Patience with Oliver. Anne had not been in the least surprised to see Oliver. Patience realized that, obviously, the two must have conceived a plan during one of their letter exchanges. No wonder Lily had been so busy in recent weeks. She was thinking of what to say when Isaac opened the front door again, this time to reveal Thomas standing there. Suddenly he was in front of her.

"Hello Patience, did you think that I'd gotten lost? Anne, I'm so sorry to be late, but Master Dudley needed me to stay and finish some important work for court tomorrow. Birthday congratulations." He put Patience's hand through his arm in a proprietary way. Standing close by, William glanced over, a quick flicker of irritation in his eyes, but his attention was brought back insistently to the lady who stood firmly in his way, speaking vigorously to him.

"We're both delighted you could come," Anne said immediately. "Oliver Mansfield, Thomas Warren of Plimouth." The men shook hands but before they could speak, a thin, heavily rouged woman who was intent on hearing every detail of Anne's accident interrupted. Patience turned to Thomas, leaving her arm where he had placed it.

"I see the Wentworths on the other side of the room. Come, I'll walk you over." They moved through the crowd to the Wentworths who were clearly pleased to see Thomas. Their conversation was cut short, however, as others moved in between them. Patience and Thomas drifted off.

"Is Oliver a close friend of Anne's?"

"Yes."

"But he's British and Master Wentworth is—"

"Stubborn," Patience finished sharply. Thomas looked startled. Patience shook her head. "I'm sorry, I didn't mean to be rude. It's just that their friendship is a definite problem. They really care for each other, but Anne's father, as you can imagine, is being very difficult about letting them see one another."

"Poor Anne. By trying to please everyone, she winds up pleasing no one. How much luckier if your heart follows a course that makes both you and your family happy." Patience could not be sure, but thought that perhaps he looked at her a trifle longer than necessary.

They walked slowly toward the front parlor, into the crush of beautiful gowns and elegant waistcoats. The twinkling candlelight sparkled off the dazzling diamonds, emeralds, and sapphires that had been taken from their velvet-lined jewelry boxes just for the occasion. She pointed out the Governor and his wife who were surrounded by a group of admirers. "Definitely Loyalist territory," Thomas observed dryly. Patience noticed that Mistress Cotton and Pamela, with a man whom she assumed was Master Cotton, were nudging their way to stand next to the Balfours. As usual, Mistress Balfour and Suzanna were both vying to be the center of attention. She smiled to herself. Some things never changed.

"Oh, there's my tutor William. Let me introduce you."

"Mmm, perhaps later, it would seem that dinner is about to be served. May I escort you?" He extended his arm and placed her hand there, curling his fingers warmly around hers.

Almost immediately, Henry, resplendent in new livery, rang the bell to announce the meal. The guests moved in a wave to the dining room and helped themselves from the extensive buffet. Roasts of venison, lamb, and pork studded with special spices, weighed heavily on the newly polished silver trays. Bountiful displays of vegetables, carefully roasted over all-day fires in the kitchen complemented the meats and relishes. A separate table of fruit-filled puddings and cakes rounded out the offerings. Cook's inventory would be substantially reduced after such a meal.

The guests took their plates and moved to places where small tables and dining chairs had been set. Patience saw Deirdre Foster and David Tremont sitting alone and brought Thomas over to them. For a moment she remembered her impression from the glimpse she had had in that Boston alley months before, that Thomas and David knew each other. But they shook hands as strangers would, and she soon forgot her initial thought. David, she found, could be quite charming when he made the effort and the four enjoyed themselves during the meal, laughing and joking about many small things.

After dinner Deirdre and David left to chat with other friends and Patience saw William standing alone. "Oh, there's William over by the fireplace. Now appears to be an good time to introduce you." She tried to gently lead Thomas in that direction. He did not move.

"Perhaps later Patience. I neglected to pass on the Dudleys' greetings to the Wentworths. I see that our host and hostess are circling the room. Let's intercept them."

She looked at him quizzically. Was he avoiding an introduction to William? That would certainly not be like him. She had been very sure that he would like to meet the tutor whom she had so often mentioned. She had developed a definite fondness for William. He was . . . well, interesting. She had been hoping to have him talk to Thomas about colonial rights, to convince him to become involved in what was happening in Boston.

Thomas' lack of interest was puzzling, but rather than making anything of it, she allowed herself to be moved into the Wentworths' path.

"The Dudleys send their regrets. They had planned to be here, but Master Dudley had an unavoidable business meeting."

"Yes, so he mentioned when last we spoke," Master Wentworth said, then added laughingly, "business matters are no respecter of social engagements."

Looking toward the front door, Mistress Wentworth waved over the crowd as William, prevented by the throng of guests from getting any closer, nodded, mouthed a good-bye, and left. Patience was disappointed. "It looks as though I'll have to meet your Master Allen at some later date, Patience," Thomas said, following her glance toward the entrance. Then, avoiding her eyes, he quickly added, "Would you all please excuse me for a moment? I see a client of Master Dudley with whom I must urgently speak." Without waiting for a reply, he slipped swiftly into the crowd, leaving Patience alone with the Wentworths. There was an abrupt silence, which Anne's mother sought to fill. "Patience dear, it seems that Governor Hutchinson is planning to hold a ball within the month. We are all being invited."

"Commanded to attend is more accurate," Master Wentworth grumbled. His wife squeezed his arm and, sensing that Patience felt a bit awkward at Thomas's sudden disappearance, asked, "Dear, would you mind trying to locate Anne and see how she's feeling? I'm concerned that she might overexert herself tonight."

Patience walked slowly through the rooms overflowing with people until she saw Anne, with Oliver hovering beside. She moved through the crowd to reach her, and relayed her mother's question. Anne laughed, "I have never felt less tired. Are you having a good time, Patience? Where are your two escorts?" Oliver raised an eyebrow at the question. Patience shrugged, but was saved from having to explain by the arrival of a talkative, elderly lady who asked insistently for the particulars about the new house in Scituate. Leaning down, Patience whispered, "I'll report back to your mother," and began to thread her way back through the crowd again, stopping to speak occasionally to the few people she had met before.

Passing one of the windows, she glanced out casually at the dormant garden, now shrouded in darkness except for a solitary lantern that illuminated a corner of the turned over herb patch. She stopped short, not believing her eyes. At the edge of the light, there among the almost bare trees and dying autumn flowers stood Thomas, waving his arms and talking with none other than William. It appeared as though their conversation was at an end for, within a few moments, Patience saw them part company, clapping each other on the shoulder as only old friends did. William left immediately and Thomas headed back toward the house.

She moved swiftly to the front hall to intercept him. She very much wanted to find out how two men who seemingly had never met before, had become so friendly so quickly.

She encountered him at the entrance. "Why Thomas," she said innocently, "I didn't realize that you needed to speak with a client outside the house."

"Oh, yes," he said, looking uncomfortable. "He was just going and I . . . I managed to catch him as he reached his carriage."

She frowned. Why didn't he simply admit that he had been talking with William? Why did he look so guilty? She looked at him closely. Was she only imagining that he was hiding something? No, she didn't think so. Something strange was going on here and she intended to find out what it was. She opened her mouth to speak, but Governor and Mistress Hutchinson, who stood near the entrance as they thanked the Wentworths loudly for a perfectly splendid evening, momentarily diverted her attention. When she turned back, Thomas had disappeared. Looking over the heads of those nearest, she saw his back twenty feet away. What was going on? She started toward him, but had walked no further than a few feet when the movement of guests heading toward the entryway stopped her. The departure of the Governor and his wife clearly signaled that the party was over. People lined up in a formal fashion to say a few carefully considered words to the Wentworths. Patience was preoccupied with her own thoughts and paid little attention, bidding an automatic farewell to even those few whom she knew well. She was surprised to see that Thomas was in the last group to go, but his good-bye was quick and said in the company of others.

After Isaac had shut the door on the last couple, she slowly climbed the stairs to her room, following the footman who was carrying Anne. She could tell that Anne was at last exhausted. She could not keep her up any longer tonight, but tomorrow she would have to talk to her about Thomas. What was happening? She hoped that Anne might have some idea.

# Chapter 10

*14 November 1773*

*Dearest Father and Mother,*

*Thank you for your letter. It arrived by coach only six days after you wrote it, so the news that Charity and Matthew have reached an understanding is still fresh. I can see why an announcement will not be made until after Prudence's wedding. I have shared the excitement with the Wentworths and they send their best wishes.*

*Truly, I am very careful when I go out in Boston. As you rightly believe, there is much feeling about the horrible tea tax (for that is what some call it). Master Wentworth has heard that certain colonial ports may refuse entrance to the tea ships. Many here, however, have ties to English merchants who say they have financed our colonial "prosperity." They say that people in England are out of work because we have not imported our fair share of their goods, and have tried to take over their trade routes. Naturally, those here who agree with them support the Crown and feel the tax is justified. Schoolmaster Allen has been giving us instruction in the history of England and her colonies. Master Wentworth has stated his views on matters too. Anne says that it is very unusual for him to let us know how he feels and she believes that he is deliberately trying to cast the British in a poor light to discourage any English friendships she has. I have tried to suggest that perhaps her father believes that we can avoid difficulties more easily if we know the source of them. As you may judge from the letter, I have been caught up in both sides of the argument.*

*At the end of the month, Governor and Mistress Hutchinson are to give a ball. The Wentworths were invited in such a public way at Anne's birthday party, that to refuse would have given grave offense. I have been invited also, and Mistress Wentworth has insisted that both Anne and I get new gowns. I told her that the green dress you made me would be fine, but she has assured me that she would be very unhappy were she not allowed to do this and that you, she is sure, would not object. I am certain that the new dress can be altered when I return home so that Charity will be able to use it as well. Mistress Wentworth has taken our measurements to Madame Toussignant, her seamstress. The result of Madame's efforts is to be a surprise.*

*Anne was most happy with my birthday gift of the silver pin. She says she will bring the piece with her when they come to Plimouth for Prudence's wedding and you will see how finely it is cut. The Wentworths' move to Scituate will take place shortly after Prudence's wedding. Some of the packing has already begun. Although Anne is most distressed at leaving her friends, I try to console her by pointing out that we will be much closer and able to see one another more often.*

*Thomas Warren stops by to walk several afternoons a week. I asked if it was not inconvenient with his job, but he said that Master Dudley is very happy to give him time off so that I can stretch my Plimouth legs safely (those are Thomas' words). Mistress Canfield has been so delighted since the news of Mistress Dunham came to her that Master Dudley feels this is a small enough service he can offer (again, Thomas' words). Thomas teases me often, but I think there must be a thread of truth in it. Indeed, I am happy to hear of the joy with which Mistress Dunham received her first letter from Mistress Canfield. It is surely a treasure to be in touch with someone who shares the same good childhood memories.*

*I must end this letter to get ready for my lessons. I have learned so much and I am surprised at how much more I seek to know. You are in my daily prayers as you have reassured me I am in yours.*

*Your loving daughter,*
*Patience*

Absentmindedly twisting one of her curls, she read over her letter, and then sealed it shut. She hoped her careful comments on the tea tax were as neutral as she had meant them to be. It would be best if her parents did not know about the worsening trouble in the city. She also knew that she should have mentioned her friendship with William, and was unable to explain, even to herself, why she had not.

She thought back to her conversation with Anne, who had been as puzzled as she that Thomas would pretend not to know William when he clearly did. "Are you sure," she had asked, "that Thomas did not say that he knew him and you just forgot?"

"I'm positive," she had countered. "He avoided him all night." Anne had been unable to come up with any other explanation.

With a start, Patience remembered she had not sent along her good wishes to the rest of the family and realized, somewhat surprised, how sincerely she meant them. Just now, she would have to hurry to be in time for lessons; she'd simply have to write again tomorrow.

Because Thomas had to go with Master Dudley to Cambridge, he would be unable see her this afternoon. William had also begged off because of a "previous commitment." His obviously deliberate lack of details about the appointment stirred an irritable curiosity.

Perhaps she would call on Deirdre, as Anne had urged her to do. She noticed that it was fast becoming a raw gray day; walking would be uncomfortable. She quickly decided that she would take Mistress Wentworth's offer of the carriage, and stopped at the writing desk to pen an invitation to Deirdre. Dropping the note off with Lily, she hurried to the open door of Anne's room.

They had kept the habit of having classes there, even though Anne was up and about in the house at other times. The doctor still insisted she have rest periods during the day and the time after lessons worked out well for that.

William was already there. She was still annoyed at his secrecy about his "previous commitment." Also, now that she reminded herself, she was also irritated with Thomas for his dishonesty about knowing William. She decided that she would treat both men coolly for the time being, starting now with the one at hand.

"I am so sorry to be late," she said, including only Anne in her smile.

"No delay at all," the teacher responded diplomatically. "I was early and Anne and I were just discussing the Crown's right to tax." Her lips tight with exasperation, Patience slid onto the chair next to the bed. Ignoring someone did no good if he didn't realize he was being ignored.

Anne's sharp response cut into her thoughts, "Not discussing at all. I was telling you that we're the King's subjects and he has a right to expect support for his protection. That is not a discussion; it is a statement of fact."

The schoolmaster began, "But what if—"

Politely, but firmly, Anne interrupted, "This whole subject tires me. It's all Boston ever talks about. Please let's take up something else—anything else."

Anne's obvious testiness erased Patience's own irritation, and she quickly asked about the pronunciation of certain French verbs. Anne, who enjoyed learning French and had a talent for it, turned her attention back to the studies and William agreeably followed.

At the end of the lesson, Anne leaned back and closed her eyes, preparing to rest a little, while Patience walked William to the Wentworths' front door. He apologized again for being unable to go with her on their usual walk.

"Is your appointment in town?" she asked coyly. William's grin let her know that her attempt to discover anything further had failed miserably. He leaned close and whispered in her ear, "Curiosity killed the cat."

She sniffed and tossed her head, ignoring his humor, and answered dismissively, "It doesn't matter to me. I was just making conversation. Mistress Wentworth has already given me the use of the carriage and Lily is bringing a note around to my friend Deirdre. I should know shortly if she's available." As if on cue, Lily stepped into the hall and handed her a slip of paper. Patience read Deirdre's response.

"There," she said defensively, doing her best to look unconcerned with William's plans. "Deirdre is free. As you can see, I am well taken care of."

She smiled brightly for effect. "Lily, please let Mistress Wentworth know I will accept her kind offer of the carriage." Regretting that a possibly interesting conversation would continue without her, Lily reluctantly left.

William observed wryly. "It is well that you have an alternative. I think my teaching here will soon end. I'm sure Anne will have much to keep her busy once she's able to move around easily again."

With instant dismay, Patience realized that he was probably right. Anne's attitude about the lessons had never been good. She would surely persuade her parents soon that she no longer needed a home tutor. That would mean that Patience too, would be saying good-bye to him. She was sharply disappointed at the prospect, and blurted out, "Soon end? Oh William, I hadn't thought of that. You've taught me so much. I shall miss you."

He placed his hand lightly on her arm. She could feel its warm impression through the sleeve of her chemise. "And I you." He looked deeply into her eyes and added, "I only wish the time was right for something more."

Glancing over her shoulder, he saw the ever-present Henry approaching. "Ah, our wraps. May I wait with you outside until the carriage arrives?" Henry started to caution that it would take some minutes to harness the horses but, sensing that the young lady might want to be alone with the young gentleman beyond the eavesdropping ears of the household, said nothing.

She nodded and William slipped into his coat. Then, taking her cloak from Henry, he placed it gently around her, and leaving his hand on her shoulder walked her outside. Henry closed the door against the chilly November wind. As they moved forward, William's arm slipped around her holding the warmth of the house between them. She was startled, but made no move to distance herself.

"My dear," he began. Then he paused, as if unsure how to proceed. "We must speak now. I am not certain we shall have another chance." Again there was a silence. She waited apprehensively. What was he going to say? At last, he seemed to reach a decision and started once more.

"Over the past few weeks I've come to see how strongly you feel about colonial rights." She turned to look at him.

"But how did you know? I thought I was being so careful. Because of Anne—"

"I know, I know. But I had hoped you would believe as I do, and I watched for the signs." His eyes stared straight ahead, but his grip on her shoulder tightened. His voice was low, and she strained to hear him against the wind. "Do you remember my speaking about my sponsor Joshua Quincy?"

She nodded, worrying what he would say next.

"As I told you, Master Quincy is a wonderful man who has been a friend of my family since long before I was born. He helped me enormously when I first came to Boston, arranging for my stay in his home, and even for pupils when I began to teach."

She interrupted. "Yes, as a matter of fact I do remember. I have also met him here a number of times. He seems to be a special friend of Master Wentworth; he seems a most intelligent, likable person."

His voice gained strength, "He is all of that, Patience, and he is also respected in the city as a devoted patriot."

Drawing her cape tighter against the damp chill of the day, she looked quizzically at him. "Well, that may well be, but what do his political views have to do with me?"

He took her hand, but continued looking straight ahead at an all but empty Salem Street. "I have never hidden my own views on the colonial cause, Patience. Like Master Quincy, I want to be thought of as a dedicated patriot." He paused again. "I am relying now on your silence." He turned, studying her. She stared back.

"I need to tell you something, something important." He mumbled to himself, "How shall I start?" Then his words rushed on, "You and I have often walked to Wheeler's Stationers. I am sure you've noticed that many times when we are there I make a trip to the back room. What you could not have known is that Wheeler's is not just a stationer's." He stopped, and looked directly at her without smiling. There could be no misunderstanding. "It is, in fact, a place where patriots meet to exchange important information." She felt her heart beat faster, as if she had raced a great distance. She was suddenly too hot; the warm cloak was suffocating her. He searched her face long and hard. "By telling you this, I have placed my complete trust and my very life in your hands. If someone who is loyal to the Crown should find out and pass the information on to the authorities, England would see it as treason. It could mean my death and the death of those closest to me." A gust of bone-chilling wind blew against them, but she did not feel it. All that William saw in her face was that she understood.

"You know I'll tell no one."

He continued in an urgent undertone. "I must ask you to do something. I have no choice." He took a deep breath, and plunged ahead. "You're recognized as someone who goes to Wheeler's regularly, who is also a member of a prominent household, still apparently friendly to the Governor. It's crucial that certain information be delivered to the stationers and, unfortunately, I've become too well known to the Loyalists. Men like Suzanna Balfour's father have been asking questions. I can't go back to the shop." His next words rang in her ears, "Your continued trips there, however, would arouse no suspicion." His hand tightened on hers. "I'm sure you know what I am asking you to do." His voice dropped, "I hope I have not made a mistake." He continued to face her without expression. He had issued a challenge.

Minutes passed in silence as she took in what he had said. Finally, she made her decision. She spoke quietly, but with no hesitation, "You are not mistaken, William, about my feelings concerning our rights in the colonies. I just need to know that anything I do will not bring trouble to the Wentworths, or to anyone else who is a friend, or to my family."

He replied quickly, eager to reassure her. "We, too, are most anxious that nothing happen to anyone who helps us, not to you, not to your friends, not to your family. We have taken every precaution to make sure that only Master Wheeler and I understand your real reason for going to his shop. If you tell no one, no one will know."

She nodded decisively. "Then no one will know." Her mind raced to plan the details.

"I will need to press Lily into service again. We have gotten out of the habit of walking together, but it shouldn't be too difficult to persuade her to start accompanying me once more." She added, with a rueful smile, "Lily is happy to have any excuse to be out of doors." She paused, "Has Master Wheeler been involved from the beginning?" She remembered so clearly that the stationer had argued about giving England the benefit of the doubt.

"From the beginning. But he felt it was important for you to see both sides of the issue and so he took up the arguments of England."

"Then you planned to ask for my help right along?"

"No, no. Master Wheeler could see that I—" He hesitated for the first time, unsure of how to word his feelings, "I liked you, and, at first, was unsure about your involvement."

"But—"

"Patience," he said firmly, "things have moved too quickly for us, personally. The future is uncertain and I have promises to fulfill. And, for now, I must be content believing you are the most trustworthy person I know. Just please, please, be careful!" His plea was followed by a wordless hug.

Just then the carriage pulled around to the front and, as Isaac jumped down to help her, William continued talking as if their conversation had been about nothing of importance. "I will see you tomorrow," he said lightly. "Enjoy your afternoon out with your friend." He squeezed her hand gently. Both understood that it was more than a casual farewell.

Once in the coach, Patience, suddenly tired, snuggled into the warmth of the blanket and deliberately put the conversation out of her mind. A few minutes and three streets later, the carriage stopped for Deirdre who readily slipped into her role as a humorous guide to some of the far-flung areas of the city. The girls enjoyed themselves thoroughly, ending up once more at Master Paul Revere's North Boston shop where Deirdre bought some silver buttons for her ball gown. "We too, will attend the Governor's ball," she said. "It would not be politic to stay away."

From the way that Deirdre's father continued to refuse to sell the English company's tea, Patience knew that he sided with Master Wentworth. She guessed that, although Master Foster walked carefully in front of those lined up with England, he would stand with the colonials if it came to a confrontation. Confrontation. She blanched at the thought. Would it come to that? She wished she could talk to Deirdre about what she was going to do, but knew that she absolutely could not. Loose talk could land William in jail or worse.

For the first time, the implications of what she had agreed to hit her full force. She shivered and deliberately spoke of something else.

"Even I have received an invitation to the Governor's," she said lightly, expecting some evidence of surprise.

"Of course," Deirdre replied matter-of-factly. "You are the honored guest of a very important Boston family. Naturally, you would be included."

Patience had never thought of herself as an honored anything. She shrugged and began to talk with Deirdre about what would be worn and who would be expected at the ball.

The following days passed uneventfully. William came to tutor and spoke hurriedly to Patience about continuing to go to Wheeler's, but gave her no information to pass. She followed his instructions and, when she walked in the afternoons with Lily, stopped at the shop to get a pen nib or some other trifle. It was not a stop, however, on her walks with Thomas.

♦ ♦ ♦

The following Saturday, she and Anne went together to the parlor for a portrait sitting. Mistress Wentworth had known immediately of a struggling artist who would gladly paint a miniature to put in Anne's pin, as well as a full-length portrait for Anne's parents. Anne rested calmly on the settee, while Patience stood behind her, shifting from one foot to the other. The artist arrived and busily set up his easel under Henry's watchful eye. Mistress Wentworth glided in and out, taking in both the preparations and the girls' behavior.

Anne giggled as she watched her friend twist again. "Patience dear, you really are not well named, although your parents undoubtedly had great hopes."

Patience smiled ruefully. Her mind jumped back to a long ago Plimouth summer day when Thomas had teased her in the same way. She had sputtered then, she remembered, "I just can't imagine sitting still," she added, "Except in church, of course." Her parents would tolerate nothing less. "How do you do it?"

"I let my thoughts take me places I can't go," Anne replied. "My body becomes still as my dreams move beyond. Actually, I've become quite good at it lately."

Patience smiled sympathetically. "I'll try it then," she said, without much hope of success.

From behind his easel, the artist gave his orders. When he was satisfied, told his subjects not to move.

Patience froze her position, and directed her thoughts to flee. They obeyed and traveled back in time a week to her pledge to William. Would she, in fact, really be called upon to help in the cause? She was no longer innocent about political matters. This was a dangerous time and it was certain that the British would fiercely resist any move toward colonial independence. Would there be war? Her brother Samuel was in the militia now. He was so young. Would he be forced into the fighting? How would her parents feel about that? She knew her mother especially had strong ideas against war and her father had even spoken from the pulpit about the evils of war. Would it come to that? How long could it last? Long enough for her younger brother Ben to be caught up in it also? That couldn't be. He was only ten, just a child. Would Oliver and William face each other across a battlefield? And what would happen to everyone, to their families and homes?

She tried to quell her escalating panic. Perhaps there could be a compromise somehow, and then peace. She deliberately put herself in a calm place.

Thomas, handsome Thomas, who could always make her laugh—she would think of him. What would happen to him if the trouble became worse? He seemed to rise above the undercurrents of danger. He seemed not to even notice them. He had no interest whatever in anything political. Where would he stand? That question had become the biggest one of all for her. She had come to like him so much that she would feel almost betrayed if he did not feel as she did about—

"That's enough for this afternoon, ladies," a voice interrupted her thoughts, bringing her insistently back to the present. "I think one more sitting the day after tomorrow and we'll be done." The artist added cheerfully, "You've been most patient." He was surprised at the burst of laughter that greeted the statement. They had seemed to be two such well-behaved young ladies.

As the girls stretched, Patience was amazed to note that two hours had gone by. "It works," she said, giving Anne a beaming smile. She was sure she would have plenty to dream about at the next session.

♦  ♦  ♦

The first call to the patriot cause came some days later. As she and William left Anne's room after yet another lesson filled with barely restrained arguments about England, he looked furtively up and down the hallway, and whispered, "Here, please take this to Master Wheeler." He thrust forward a folded sheet of white paper, sealed with a wax impression. She stared at the note without moving. "Patience," he said insistently, "put it away quickly. Someone might see us."

Dreamlike, she slowly opened her hand. Suddenly, there was the sound of footsteps coming up the stairs. She grabbed the note and tucked it nervously into the waistband of her skirt, just as Lily came into view, a cup of hot chamomile tea in her hand.

"Oh, hello, there," Patience prattled anxiously, her voice unnaturally high. "How are you this afternoon? We've just finished a wonderful lesson, and I am walking Master Allen downstairs. After you've taken Anne her tea, perhaps we can go for our afternoon walk. You are free, aren't you?"

She felt overwhelmingly hot; perspiration trickled down her neck and her cheeks flushed as they always did when she was nervous. She was suddenly and acutely aware of how she must sound, and closed her mouth with great effort, lest any more silly babble escape. Lily looked at her curiously, but merely answered formally in front of the teacher, "Yes, Miss Patience. Cook'll let me go anytime," and passed on to the room. The maid, absorbed with curiosity ever since Patience and the schoolmaster had stopped their daily walks, paused near the door, straining to hear what the two were talking about, but to no avail.

As soon as Lily had gone into Anne's room and shut the door after her, William looked at Patience in dismay. He touched her arm, "Are you sure you want to do this? You seem terribly upset."

She took a deep breath, and answered in an almost normal voice, "I'm fine, truly. I was simply startled. I have the note secure and all will be well." They walked together in silence to the front door, seeing no one except Henry, who waited by the entrance with William's coat.

Once bundled against the autumn wind, William tipped his hat and said loudly enough for the disappearing Henry to overhear, "Good day, Patience, I shall see you and Anne tomorrow. It may be wise for both of you to practice the past tense of those French verbs. Practice makes perfect you know."

Then he was gone, leaving her to her first mission.

She took a deep breath, squared her shoulders, and walked decisively up the stairs to her room, where she transferred the note, unread, to the hidden pocket of her cloak. For an instant she regretted that the wax sealed its contents from her eyes, but then was almost relieved that it did. She wrapped herself protectively in the cloak and tied her bonnet securely, checking her appearance carefully in the mirror. Except for the slightly heightened color still remaining in her cheeks, she looked the same as she always did. Now, if her heart would just stop thundering, she would be fine.

Lily, also clothed against the bleak November day, knocked lightly on the door, and the girls proceeded out of the safe haven of the Wentworth home. Patience knew that all had to appear normal, lest Lily suspect anything out of the ordinary and say as much to Anne. With that in mind, she kept up an inane chatter the entire way to the center of town, blithering on about every inconsequential thing she could think of. As they approached the vicinity of Wheeler's, Lily interrupted. "Oh, look, there's Miss Suzanna's father. My, doesn't he look grand."

"Where?" Patience asked sharply. She had to avoid as many Loyalists, as possible. She was nervous enough without running into those who could make her more so.

"There, by Wheeler's. He's talking to those men."

Master Balfour and two others blocked the steps to the stationers. Why were they there? She could see no obvious reason for them to be standing by the side of the entrance. Were they suspicious of those who went in Wheeler's? Could they be checking? Slowing the path of her approach, she studied them carefully. As she and Lily drew near, the three men seemed to be involved only in their own conversation, paying no attention to what was around them. Then just as she was about to mention casually to Lily that she really should stop in for more writing paper, she saw Master Balfour suddenly look hard at a man who stepped around him to enter the shop. The trio ceased talking. Oh no! They were checking Master Wheeler's customers. Her heart stopped and she frantically searched for an alternative. Concentrating on keeping her voice even, she said "Lily, let's cross over to Madame Toussignant's. I want to ask her about the bodice tucking on Suzanna's chemise. I really don't understand how it's done and I'm sure she can explain it to me." She took the maid's arm insistently and hurried her across the street to the seamstress' small and exclusive shop. She had met its owner at the Wentworths' on numerous occasions and had found the woman, a long ago French transplant, snobbish and overbearing, an opinion that was irrelevant just now.

The doorbell rang stridently as the girls entered the shop. The counters of the front room overflowed with bolts of material of every color and hue. A jumble of half completed garments hung on hooks along the back wall. The room's two chairs had been set at an angle to share the poor light struggling to come through the window. The chairs' occupants, pale, thin girls close to the ages of Patience's younger brothers, did not look up, but continued to industriously ply their needles in tiny perfect stitches on the blue brocade material slung across their laps. Madame herself peeked out from the back room and, noting a potential customer, bustled forward to be of assistance.

"Hello Madame Toussignant," Patience said brightly. "I'm not sure if you remember me. I'm—"

"But of course I do. You're staying at the Wentworths. Miss Burgess isn't it?"

"Yes Madame. I was passing by and remembered I wished to inquire about the exquisite tacking you did on my friend Suzanna Balfour's chemise." She continued swiftly, mindful of Lily's puzzled frown, and hoping that the mention of Suzanna's name would loosen the Frenchwoman's tongue. "I was trying to describe it in my latest letter to my mother and was quite unable to do so."

Preening at the compliment, the seamstress moved closer. "Why thank you Miss Burgess. It was rather difficult to perfect the technique." As Madame Toussignant described the procedure, complimenting herself in the same breath, Patience managed to maneuver her position so that she had a clear view of the front of Wheeler's. Automatically making the proper responses to the details of the sewing feat, she carefully observed what was happening across the street.

A steady stream of customers entered the popular store. After several minutes, it was apparent that, while Master Balfour and his companions looked carefully at each man who went through Wheeler's front door, they scarcely glanced at any woman who entered there. Patience took a breath to steady herself. She could manage this. Without caring that the seamstress was only part way through a detailed recital of stitching and tucking, she smiled widely and interrupted. "Thank you so much for telling me how you accomplish such a complicated design. I'm sure Mistress Wentworth will be pleased you took the time. Be assured I shall tell her of your help." She took Lily's hand firmly, and without a

backward glance, led her through the door, leaving Madame
Toussignant puzzled and irritated that she had not been accorded
her full measure of deference.

Walking down the shop steps, Patience said, as if it had just
occurred to her, "Oh Lily, I remember that I need some of that
new stationery Master Wheeler has received. Let's stop by now
since we are here." Lily had not even finished nodding agreeably
before she was rushed across the street and up another set of
steps. Patience, with a deliberate smile on her face, turned toward
the trio of men standing by the entrance. "Good day, Master
Balfour." The men tipped their hats automatically and Master
Balfour harrumphed.

"Good day Miss—mmm—Miss—" Perfect. He had
completely forgotten who she was. She whisked Lily through the
door, and breathed an audible sigh of relief. Now she just needed
to find a moment alone with Master Wheeler.

"Lily, we seem to be running short of time. Would you please
pick up that rose stationery for me, ten sheets I think, while I just
get a book waiting for me in the back." She handed the maid a ten
pence coin.

Lily ambled over to get the attention of one of the clerks
while Patience headed quickly toward the back room.
Fortunately, Master Wheeler was standing alone behind a pile of
books. He looked up, immediately understood why she was there,
and glanced around. No one was in the vicinity. He picked up one
of the books in front of him and pushed it into her outstretched
hand. "Ah Miss Burgess, so good of you to be so prompt in
picking up your order." He continued genially, "That will be one
pound six, I believe." She handed him the sum with the secret
note folded beneath. He promptly tucked both into his pocket.
Hearing footsteps, they turned simultaneously just as Lily
rounded the corner, a wrapped parcel in her hand.

Patience smiled at Master Wheeler and said, "Thank you so
much for meeting my order. I have waited for this book a long
time." She glanced at the cover. It was a treatise of inspirational
sermons, soon, she decided, to be a gift for Prudence's intended.
"Because I write home often you can be assured I shall be a
steady customer for your lovely stationery." They both offered

polite farewells, and Patience and Lily retraced their steps to the front of the store and departed. The Loyalists were gone. The girls walked back up Salem Street to the Wentworth residence. Patience could not wait to get to her room. She was exhausted.

♦ ♦ ♦

At the conclusion of a late November lesson, Master Wentworth came unexpectedly to Anne's room. "William, when you have finished with the girls' lesson, would you please stop by my study."

"Of course sir," William answered respectfully, exchanging a glance with Patience.

Minutes later, the lesson was completed and William was on his way to see Master Wentworth. Patience was anxious. "I wonder why your father wants to see William."

If Anne knew, and Patience strongly suspected that she did, she pretended ignorance and both girls waited for the result of the discussion.

It took less than twenty minutes for Schoolmaster Allen to be given notice that his services would no longer be required. He walked stoically up the stairs to say good-bye to his pupils. Anne was polite, correct as always, "Thank you so much, William, for the months of lessons. I know that I sometimes appeared a less than interested pupil, but I do appreciate the time that you have spent tutoring us." She offered her hand, which he took and shook briefly.

"Anne, the time has been profitably spent, I hope." He turned to Patience who quickly put out her hand.

"Thank you for everything William. I've enjoyed our time together."

He smiled at her. "The pleasure, Patience, has been all mine." And then he was gone. Patience was sad to see him leave. She would miss the excitement he brought to her studies, the challenge to look beyond the usual. She would miss him too.

Days passed, and suddenly the time for the Governor's ball was at hand. Anne could not contain her happiness. She would be seeing Oliver again. Her parents could do little to prevent it, although they had made it clear he was not to call at the house any longer. Anne told Patience that with her injured leg soon healed, she would be able to see Oliver at places away from home. Although her father had made definite plans to move the family to Scituate after the first of the year, Anne refused to worry further about it, saying her wonderful Oliver would think of something.

On the afternoon of the ball, Madame Toussignant herself came to help dress the ladies, declaring, "I wish my gowns to be displayed to the best advantage." Patience laughed at the dressmaker's arrogance, but took her turn being pulled and prodded, tucked and laced, until all was declared in order.

With nothing left to do until it was time to go, she presented herself at Anne's door, with Madame Toussignant's warning not "to sit and wrinkle" still ringing in her ear. Anne had been dressed earlier so that she could rest until the moment of departure. Entering the room, Patience saw the sparkle in her eyes, no doubt in anticipation of seeing Oliver again.

"Ah, Patience. You look like a princess," Anne said sincerely. "Thomas will have to guard you well or someone will dance off with you."

Patience blushed at the compliment and smiled at the thought of Thomas seeing her in such finery. She had long ago forgotten her intention to treat him coolly. He would be attending with the Dudleys, so he had told her, and expected her to save him several dances. She twirled slowly, the icy blue colored underskirt on the stiffened silk dress sparkled with brillants as they caught the lamp light. The darker aquamarine overskirt was elegant, not with ruffles—"that wouldn't do at all," Madame Toussignant had declared authoritatively—but draped gently over the lighter blue.

"I have just the thing to complete your ensemble," Anne said, taking out a string of garnets from the velvet jewelry case on the bedside table.

"Oh, I couldn't," Patience said.

"You must! Then I shall be able to wear the diamonds I received for my birthday, for I have lent you this."

"But—" Patience began.

"Indeed, it is the very thing," Anne stated firmly, motioning Patience over to fasten the garnets behind her neck. "Father will be delighted when everyone sees his good taste in jewelry at both our throats." She giggled and Patience realized how little Anne had laughed this past month.

"I shall keep my hand over it all night," she promised, fingering the delicate necklace to reassure herself of its continued presence.

"Don't concern yourself. Father made sure it had a very good clasp. It was for my fifteenth birthday and I was somewhat uncontrollable then." They both laughed. Fifteen was a very long time ago.

The ball had already begun by the time the Wentworth party entered the Governor's home in Milton. Everyone made a great fuss over Anne, making sure she was seated just so on the settee. She was flushed and whispered to Patience that she had hoped to be able to sit quietly without attention at the edge of the ballroom. Patience responded that she would have been able to do so had she not looked so outstanding. Anne smiled, but Patience knew she was waiting impatiently until Oliver could come over to her. As they had left the house Master Wentworth, increasingly upset by all things British and, more immediately, by the arrival of the tea ships in Boston Harbor, had declared, "We will stay only as long as propriety dictates." No one had dared offer even the slightest objection to his determination. Anne intended to spend as much time as possible with Oliver before her father took them home.

The Wentworths left the girls and went to pay their respects to Governor and Mistress Hutchinson. Patience glanced around the ballroom, which was more immense than any room for dancing she had ever seen. The walls were covered with gold tinted brocade and floral designs in the same shade of gold had been stenciled on the draperies by artisans. Matching upholstered chairs were set in conversation groups around the room, with footmen stationed nearby to fetch and carry as needed. The setting was indeed grand. At the same time, she knew that the money that went into building such splendor was unknown to most people in either Plimouth or Boston or, for that matter, in any of the other colonies. She was about to say so when she realized that Anne might not appreciate the comment. A blur of color caught her eye and she saw Thomas striding toward them.

Anne whispered, "Thomas just arrived with the Dudleys and looked for you right away."

"You can't know that," Patience whispered back.

"Yes I can. I watched," Anne replied, giggling outright.

"And what were you watching, Miss Wentworth?" Thomas asked in a light tone, as he appeared in front of them.

"Why all the lovely ball gowns, of course," she responded swiftly.

"The loveliest of all are being worn by the two ladies in this corner."

"Thank you, kind sir," Anne replied laughingly. The three of them discussed the evening for several minutes until Thomas invited Patience to dance.

"I have already received permission from Master Wentworth," he said.

"Do dance, Patience," Anne urged. "I see Mistress Balfour heading toward us and this is your only escape."

"You make it impossible to refuse," Patience said, placing her hand on Thomas' arm.

"If Plimouth could see the minister's daughter now," he teased, as they walked toward the crowded dance floor.

Patience was startled. "Do you think I look unseemly?" she asked anxiously, lifting up the pleating of her gown slightly to look at the delicate work.

"I think you look lovely," he stated firmly. "I only meant that you look every inch a fine lady."

"Oh." She could think of no further reply.

He took her hand firmly in his and they began to move in time to the music. She could feel the material of his jacket through her thin gloves and the muscles of his shoulder beneath that. She was both excited and nervous at being this close and tried desperately to think of something to say.

Fortunately he spoke first, a bit huskily. "For a fine young lady you are certainly much easier to talk to than others I could name. So many seem oblivious to what is happening here in the city."

"What happens is important to us all. Even from Plimouth my parents ask for news."

Thomas was surprised, "You write to your parents about the problems here?"

"Of course. They always ask how things are in Boston."

"How unusual."

"You don't approve?" She stiffened.

"On the contrary, I think it's very important that all of us understand what goes on. I can see you have grown up in many ways. You're not the girl I knew in Plimouth."

"That Patience is gone forever," she responded coolly as she glanced over toward Anne. Oliver had joined Anne and it looked as if they were in the midst of a serious conversation. From across the room the Wentworths had also noticed them talking and now were proceeding quickly toward the seated couple.

"I think it's time I went back to Anne," Patience said, looking at Thomas with determination. Noting the tone in her voice, he moved off the dance floor immediately and led her back toward Anne and Oliver. As she approached them, seconds before the arrival of the Wentworths, she began to talk in an artificially loud voice, trying to signal Anne that her parents were nearby.

"Yes, it is a bit warm in here, don't you think so, Anne?" Anne and Oliver moved apart. He looked distraught, and she was on the verge of tears.

Anne spoke haltingly. "You're both in time for some horrible news." She gulped. "A dreadful accident. It is truly unbelievable. Oliver's father and his brother have both been killed. A runaway carriage hit them right in the street in front of the Parliament building." She stifled a sob. "Oliver must return home to console his family and . . . and . . . take his position as Earl of Mansfield."

Patience and Thomas were shocked. But before either could say anything, Master Wentworth, close enough to have overheard, expressed his condolences. "So sorry to hear of your loss, Lord Mansfield. This must be a trying time for your family. Under the circumstances, I presume you will have to depart for England immediately."

"Yes sir," Oliver replied stoically, turning to Anne's father, "I must be on the next ship. But the governor has promised to keep my post open. I'll return when circumstances permit."

"Ah, yes . . . well, I'm sure you mean to," was Master Wentworth's response. "Please accept our sympathy for your loss." He quickly added, "And that of your family, of course. Now, we too must depart, if only to Salem Street. Anne is much too tired to stay any longer." Throughout her father's conversation Anne sat in shocked silence. Patience was quiet too, painfully aware of her feelings.

Master Wentworth helped his daughter to her feet and, with her leaning heavily on his arm, shepherded the women pointedly toward the door. Trying unsuccessfully to catch Patience's eye, Thomas waved halfheartedly after them. The Wentworth party departed for their carriage and home.

After being helped out of her gown, Patience knocked on Anne's door and entered the room. She found Anne sobbing into her pillow and went over to hold her, "Oh Patience, he said it would only be a few months, six months at most. He said he'd come back for me. But what if he doesn't?" she cried. "What if he doesn't?"

# Chapter 11

Pausing at the connecting door, Patience reflectively traced the carved outline of the sailing ship with her fingers. She knew that she would not have had the same hesitation in entering Anne's room before. But then, there had been nothing to be reluctant about. Now, with Oliver gone, Anne had withdrawn completely from everyone. She talked only when spoken to and otherwise stared out the window for hours at a time. Something had to be done. Patience knocked, and without waiting for an answer, walked in.

Anne lay back listlessly against the headboard, her face gray and drawn, Forcing an uncomfortably broad smile, Patience spoke with artificial cheerfulness, "Anne, it's finally sunny again. Let's go for a nice long walk."

Anne looked up without interest. "I don't want—" she began in a low monotone.

Patience quickly interrupted, deliberately misinterpreting her objection. "Of course, if you don't feel I can handle the chair, we can have one of the footmen come with us."

"No, no," she responded dully, taking the path of least resistance. "It would be easier for me if we were alone."

"Fine," Patience said, forcing herself to keep the lilt in her voice. "I'll call Lily."

Twenty minutes later, a strong footman on each side of the chair kept it perfectly balanced during the negotiation down the steep front stairs.

"This is a fine idea," Anne's mother said, hovering in the background, "but mind you don't catch a chill. These December winds can come up from the bay so suddenly."

"We will be fine, Mistress Wentworth," Patience replied, carefully fastening the loop of her cape. "And we shall come home as soon as either one of us feels the cold." She gripped the wooden handles at the back of the chair and started pushing it carefully down Salem Street.

They had passed by only a few houses when Anne said, "Perhaps this will make me feel better. It's just that my parents don't understand. They think with Oliver no longer here, I'll simply turn to other friends again." She sighed deeply and turned in her chair. "You do know it won't be like that, don't you?"

"Yes," Patience answered, patting her shoulder comfortingly. "I know you were truly in love."

"Am, Patience, am. There will never be anyone for me but Oliver."

Patience fervently hoped that Oliver felt as strongly. Did he miss Anne as much? She couldn't guess; she hadn't in fact gotten to know him at all. Her own feelings about him had been totally colored by his closeness to the Governor and by the way he had behaved toward that poor boy months before. Had his duty demanded that of him? She didn't know. She said nothing about that, however, and instead, for the first part of the trip around the Mall, tried to take Anne's mind off her misery.

"You should have seen him, Anne," she giggled in the middle of a story, "he had the most comical look on his face as he landed in the puddle in front of the draper's shop, beaver hat in hand. And the pig that caused the mishap strolled nonchalantly back up the street under the eye of its embarrassed keeper."

She stopped as she spied Deirdre coming out of Master Wheeler's shop. She had not been by the house in several days and even Anne was happy to wave her over. Deirdre dashed across the street, narrowly avoiding a patch of early ice on the walkway.

"Anne," she said, a trifle out of breath, "and Patience. How delightful to find you here. I had not thought you would be out with all this tea ship business."

Patience shook her head slightly, trying to warn Deirdre off the topic of the Dartmouth. The English ship, along with two others, all crammed with tea, had finally reached Boston, and was currently tied up at Griffith's Wharf. Master Wentworth had gone on at length about the situation the night before last. "Margaret," he had said, plunging his fork into the venison and glancing sideways down the table at his wife, "there's been an enormous—why, the numbers were beyond all expectations—gathering at the South Meeting House about this blasted—excuse my language—tea. It was the other night, that day I had to be in Scituate about the new ship." He had sounded extremely disappointed not to have been on hand. Anne had turned pale and clutched the edge of the table. He had chewed the venison excruciatingly slowly as those around the table waited for his next words.

"Joshua—Quincy not Burke—told me that it ended with a firm resolution that the tea will not be allowed on Boston soil. They'll make sure those provisions don't wind up on the planks of our city piers." He had taken several mouthfuls of squash while those around him had been unable to chew any food at all. "Those agents hovering about won't get a crack at the goods. That Edward Cotton is just waiting to sell that blasted—excuse me—stuff for those East India people; he can practically taste the profit. James, I'll have a bit more of the wine." He had gulped down the red liquid. "I've heard tell that the Captain of the Dartmouth, that Rotch fellow, wants to avoid trouble by sailing the cargo back to England." He had paused to look around the table.

Patience sensed that he had chosen the topic and his words with some deliberation. "Seems like a sensible enough idea." He had resumed eating, the only one at an otherwise motionless table. "But what's his name, that old customs collector, has refused to grant clearance for him to sail unless the tea's unloaded. Says he's only following the Governor's orders. What can that man be thinking!" It had been unnecessary to guess which man had caught his ire. "So far, nothing has happened, but seems to me, it's only a matter of time. Everyone knows the Sons of Liberty met at the Green Dragon to organize resistance. I think I'm about finished, James. I'll try some of that pudding."

He had looked around again. "Good heavens, has no one eaten? It's a sin to waste so much good food." The rest of the meal, which had consisted of watching him finish the molasses pudding, was completed in total silence. Thereafter Anne, looking sick, had gone immediately to her room. Patience had raced into Henry's pantry to grab the Gazette from the bottom shelf where Master Wentworth always left it when he was finished reading. With no one in sight, she had quickly skimmed the paper. There had been another of those letters signed by the anonymous Vindex advocating a tough colonial stand against England. The Gazette editor had reported that tension was high. The presence of the Sixty-fifth Regiment, as well as one other, quartered close by at Castle William ever since Crown revenue officers had been threatened, was a constant reminder of England's position in the city. She had just known there was going to be trouble.

Anne had not left her bed since that night. Now Patience held her breath to see how she would answer Deirdre. But Anne only replied primly, "The law will prevail, I am sure, and the tea will be brought ashore."

Deirdre and Patience exchanged glances. It was obvious that Anne did not understand the extent of resistance to the British forcing the tea on Boston.

Patience changed the subject quickly, "But you haven't heard the good news. The doctor said that Anne's leg is almost completely mended and that she will be able to walk on her own within days. In fact, he's going to remove the strapping in a few days, on the eighteenth. She'll be as good as new by Christmas."

Deirdre reached down and hugged Anne, "I'm so happy for you! And will you be able to do everything as before?"

"Yes," was her answer, the relief obvious, "only I must do it all more slowly at first until I get used to moving on two legs again." She looked briefly more excited than she had since Oliver left. Then her face fell. "Unfortunately, it also means the end to Patience's stay with us. That's the unhappy part of all this. I don't know what I would have done without her."

Deirdre's pretty face clouded as she turned to Patience. "That is a disappointment. I do hope we may write and visit each other."

"Oh yes. Definitely. Plimouth is not so far, and Master Wentworth has promised that there will be plenty of trips there from Scituate. Perhaps you can spend time in both places."

"You may count on that. And when will you be leaving?"

"Master Wentworth has arranged it also for the eighteenth. I'll miss seeing Anne take her first steps."

In truth, she was very anxious about leaving. She worried constantly about Anne who seemed to be growing more miserable with each passing day. She also knew that she was leaving Boston at a time when William and Master Wheeler might be counting on her. She had not yet been able to tell either one of her departure. Now she saw the chance.

"Since we are here at the stationer's, I do remember something I must pick up," she said as offhandedly as she could.

"Please stop in," Anne urged. "Deirdre and I will keep one another company."

Quickly, Patience went across the street, entered the shop, and picked up a pennyweight of yellow sealing wax. She approached Master Wheeler who was standing alone as he straightened a shelf of inking supplies. "Sir," she began in a hurried undertone, "I've just found out I'm to return home in a week's time. Master Wentworth and my father have already decided. There's no way I can delay." She looked at him anxiously. He groaned in frustration. "I don't believe this piece of bad luck. The timing couldn't be worse. England has said the tea has to be brought ashore. You know we can't let that happen. If the Governor doesn't let the ships return to England with that tea, there will be trouble." He thought hard while Patience held her breath. "We will simply have to make do. We may need you just before you leave for Plimouth." She nodded and he, suddenly understanding that, in a few days, she would be gone for good, took her hand. "Patience, we will all be most sorry to see you go," She looked at the kind face, now so familiar, and was instantly sad. She nodded again, knowing that there was really nothing further to say, then left, before Deirdre and Anne came to look for her.

The sun had disappeared behind a cloud, and Anne began to shiver in the cold. With reminders to see each other within a few days, the girls headed home. It was a quiet walk back to Salem Street. Anne was depressingly silent again.

Patience decided that she had to speak to Mistress Wentworth, even though she knew Anne would not like it. Now that William no longer came to the house, there was no one else to talk to. Thomas Warren had called upon her only once since the ball. They had walked briefly through the neighboring streets, but he had seemed distracted and they both had had a hard time finding something to say. She had been to blame too. They had left the Governor's ball so abruptly. She had been too upset by the news of the death of Oliver's father to offer even a proper farewell, let alone say anything more. Now it was even harder to flirt and tease about silly things. She could not concentrate on any friendship when she was worried about more serious matters. Resolutely, she put Thomas out of her thoughts.

As they neared the Wentworths, two footmen come swiftly down the steps to help with the chair. Anne said softly, "I think I'll just lie down a little. Please don't trouble yourself to come up. Lily can help me."

"Oh, but it's never any trouble."

"No Patience, I prefer it this way. Please."

Patience watched her being carried up the stairs. After placing her cloak in Henry's outstretched hands, she went in search of Mistress Wentworth. The lady of the house was sitting peacefully at her desk, catching up on correspondence. Patience stood quietly at the doorway until noticed.

"My dear, I'm so glad to see you back safely. With all this tea ship trouble, I worry much more when you girls are out. I trust you had a good walk."

"Yes, ma'am. We stopped to speak with Deirdre, and Anne seemed to enjoy the time." She stopped, and then gathered her resolve and plunged ahead, "I feel I must let you know how worried I am about her. Ever since Oliver—"

"Yes, yes, well—" Mistress Wentworth seemed to anticipate what she would say and interrupted somewhat testily. "I know you're concerned, Patience, but I do feel I know my own daughter quite well. She had a silly infatuation over that young man, but that is all over now. Soon she will be up and about, visiting again with her friends, and involved in the move to our lovely new home. Her father and I are convinced she will soon forget someone who is a continent away."

"I am afraid—" Patience pressed, surprised at Mistress Wentworth's insistent tone.

"Nonsense, nonsense, child," she replied, standing up to put her arm around Patience's shoulder. "I can see you're uneasy about the situation, but you need not be. It will work out shortly." She gave a decisive nod of her head.

With that unpleasant topic put aside, Mistress Wentworth went on, "I am sure you know how much we have valued your presence for these many months. I have just now written to your parents thanking them again for allowing you to stay with us. You have been a wonderful support to us all." She squeezed Patience's shoulder warmly, and Patience responded with an obedient smile, trying to put her nagging doubt aside. Perhaps Anne's mother was right; it could be that she was fretting unnecessarily. In any event there was obviously nothing she could do but write Anne often from Plimouth, lending her a sympathetic ear. The Wentworths would be there within the month for Prudence's wedding, and then Anne and she would have time to talk more about everything. A month was a long time. Perhaps by then the Wentworths would realize how much Oliver meant to Anne and would allow them to write, or perhaps Mistress Wentworth's prediction would come true and, as unlikely as it now seemed, time and distance would have cooled Anne's feeling for the Englishman.

As the time quickly drew near when the standoff over the tea ships in the harbor had to end, tempers ran high among the people of Boston and beyond. Patience had received more than one letter from Mistress Dunham bringing her up to date on the news of Plimouth. At the end of the last note she had written that there had been a town meeting and a report given concerning the "East India Company's Import of Tea into America subject to the duty payable here for raising a revenue against our consent." The letter had gone on to say that those reporting, including James Warren Esq., Thomas' father, "Expressed the firm resolution not only to oppose this step as dangerous to the liberty and commerce of this country, but also to aid and support all our brethren in their opposition to this and every violation of our rights." Mistress Dunham had ended by warning Patience to take care.

Patience did not need the warning. She was only too aware of what was happening. On every street corner, in every tavern, at every church meeting, people argued about the tea and the tax, and what would happen if the tea were not allowed to be unloaded and delivered to the agents for sale. Just yesterday she had overheard a man say, "The Frenchies'll support us in every event. After ol' King John took over Quebec, they can't wait to see 'em fall," Were there other countries that would take sides? Would more British soldiers come? She thought again about Thomas. Did he know that his father had spoken out against the tax? Thomas had seemed surprised that she wrote her parents about what she saw and heard in Boston. Maybe the Warrens never talked about such things; maybe Thomas felt differently from the rest of his family. How difficult that would be. Even though her own mother had been born and raised in England, she believed that her parents too, would agree with Plimouth's resolution. But what if Thomas truly didn't care, or didn't care to be involved in what was happening? Patience knew that she had become too passionate about the cause to accept such indifference.

One cold December evening, Master Wentworth gathered his entire household in the parlor after the evening meal. He looked sternly at them all. "It was most unpleasant at the Bull 'n Finch Tavern last night. It was divided into camps right at the entrance and there was more than one bloody fight. No one in this house is to go out alone. Anne, Patience, mind what I say! Even Salem Street has had its share of fighting over this infernal tea." Everyone in the parlor, family and servants alike, nodded in respectful obedience. Patience looked over at Anne's stoic expression. It was impossible to tell what she was thinking.

♦ ♦ ♦

On December 15th, the Collector of Customs again refused to grant clearance for the ships to leave. The gossip was that Rotch, fearing for the safety of his ship, was riding to Milton to try to secure the right of passage from the Governor himself. Late that morning, Patience received a note from William. The tutor had started writing letters to her as soon as he had left the Wentworths, saying that he needed a way of contacting her that would arouse no suspicion. By now, the household was used to the notes, and believed that he was writing to his former student about mutual academic interests. This note, however, like none of the others, was short and difficult to understand for anyone except her. It said, "We may have need of you soon. Please be available. W.A."

She waited.

◆  ◆  ◆

December 16th came. At the South Meeting House, Samuel Adams, a leader of the Sons of Liberty and the much quoted Vindex of the Gazette, along with almost seven thousand Boston followers, stood by to hear the Governor's decision about Rotch's request. If permission was granted to take the tea back to England, the immediate tension caused by the ships would be over. Master Wentworth ordered the members of his household not to go out for any reason. Patience continued to wait.

The sun was setting in the late afternoon sky when Lily came to her room. She held a crumpled note tightly in her hand. "Please Patience, a man came to the back door and said that this was for you, and you only he said." She handed her the sealed letter and craned her neck to see if she could glimpse any of the words. "Is it from that nice Thomas Warren?" She had not seen Thomas visit lately and had hoped in her romantic soul that he was back again.

Patience scanned the note quickly and saw the other smaller one enclosed. "Yes Lily it is, and I must go to see him now." She held the notes tightly and prayed that God would forgive her this one small lie. She needed Lily's help and knew she liked the handsome Master Warren.

"But...but, don't you remember? Master Wentworth himself said that no one's to go out. It isn't safe he said."

"I know, but I'll be well protected. Thomas is meeting me just outside."

"Master Wentworth . . . if he caught you. I don't know . . ." Patience waited anxiously, shifting from one foot to the other. Finally the maid decided to further the cause of romance. "We have to hurry. He's in the study with some men, but they won't be there long."

Patience ran upstairs to her room and dressed hurriedly in her cloak, making sure that William's secret instructions were secure in the concealed inner pocket. She peeked apprehensively into the hallway; no one was in sight. She tiptoed down the nearby servants' staircase that ended in the kitchen. Her luck held! Only Lily was by the open back door, rubbing her hands together from the cold, looking guilty and afraid. "I don't see Thomas. Are you sure you'll be safe?"

"Yes, Lily. I'm certain I'll be fine."

She had taken a step toward the door when suddenly she heard Henry's raised voice close by. "'Lily, are you in the kitchen?" The girls froze, but Lily recovered fast. "I'll catch him in the pantry," she whispered urgently, "you sneak out, then I'll come back later and lock the door." The maid moved swiftly through the connecting pantry, calling out, "I'm coming, I'm coming right now." Patience crept out the service entrance and huddled behind the prickly holly bush. She held her breath as Henry, with Lily in tow, stalked past the kitchen window toward the door. He opened it angrily and looked outside. "Lily, why is this door unlocked? You know Master Wentworth's order that everything is to be closed up tight. Have you been visiting with the Colt's Matthew again?" He slammed the door and clicked the lock firmly. Patience felt terrible, Lily was going to be in trouble because of her. She waited behind the holly a few more minutes, then she looked over the windowsill into the kitchen. The room was empty. She dashed into the street.

It was frigidly cold. Her breath hung in the air as she hurried through the ever-increasing number of people on the paths, "the common folk" in whom the Governor had said that he had so little faith. She knew they waited word about Rotch's last effort. She anxiously fingered the concealed slip of paper and walked rapidly through the crowded streets, shoving here and darting there, her rudeness amazing even to her. Just before she reached the stationer's shop, she ran breathlessly into a narrow alley. There was no one in sight. Her curiosity had to be satisfied. She took the note from her pocket, carefully lifted the wax seal, and read the scribbled words. They swam before her eyes. She took a deep breath to control her trembling and hastily resealed the paper. She raced out of the alley and arrived at the bottom of the steps of the stationer's shop. She forced herself to slow down. She must not arouse suspicion. She moved as unobtrusively as she could, up the worn steps, through the door, and to the counter where Master Wheeler stood.

"Some pen nibs please," she said, her voice shaking slightly. Without taking his eyes from her face, he reached into the side cupboard, located a tiny package, and passed it to her. He turned to call his apprentice as she held out the money to pay for the purchase.

"Ziekiel, I need to run an errand. Watch the shop for me."

Then the owner of the stationer's shop turned back, took the payment and the note hidden beneath the money, and said clearly, "Thank you for everything Miss Patience." He gave her a salute.

She smiled slightly. "Good-bye, Master Wheeler." Back on the street, she shoved the small decoy package filled with worthless scraps into her cloak pocket and gulped of the icy air. The deed was done. She leaned faintly against the side of the closest building and forced herself to take slow, regular breaths. Almost immediately she began to feel vibrant and alive. She walked purposefully through the crowded streets. Her mission was complete; her part was over. But she found that she was now strangely reluctant to return to the Wentworth house, safe harbor though it was. There was an atmosphere in the city such as she had never felt before. People milled about and she heard snatches of "Ol' Sam Adams," and "ain't drunk tea in forever." She knew that everyone awaited Rotch's return with the governor's decision. Unlike New York, Philadelphia, or Charleston, the Boston agents to whom the tea had been shipped had not resigned their offices to avoid trouble. That was not surprising as two of them were Governor Hutchinson's own sons. But their refusal had added fuel to the fire.

Samuel Adams, his trembling hands folded tightly together, waited at the Meeting House, along with thousands of followers. Patience stood at the outskirts of the crowd. Then word spread that Rotch was seen nearing Boston. At last someone, an older, white-haired man who looked like Saint Nicholas, elbowed his way through the throng and spoke to Adams, who took a breath, then rose and addressed them all. "This meeting can do nothing more to save the country." The crowd roared as they understood. Rotch had been denied a permit to sail.

In the streets, news of the Governor's stand spread like wildfire and with it, word that "Mohawk Indians" were headed toward the waterfront and the ships. Those who had shoved in around her now trapped Patience, who was suddenly afraid and anxious to get home. Frantic, she tried to angle her body around the fat man who blocked her way. Escape was impossible. Fear gripped her as she was pushed toward the wharf. She could feel the cobblestones beneath her boots, but the noisy human mass around her was so crushing that she could see nothing but gray woolen cloaks and scarves. She felt elbows and shoulders, and then a shove from behind. She smelled the dank, slightly salty smell of harbor water. She was prodded forward and, panicked that she would be trampled, forced herself to keep up with those nearest her. Unable to move on her own, she could concentrate on nothing but staying on her feet.

Suddenly the crowd halted at the edge of a row of piers. When the jostling stopped, she was in the forefront, sweating and disheveled as she hung desperately to one of the splintering wooden columns. She looked up with wide, astonished eyes just in time to see the "Indians" surging forward toward the cargo ships. Men, stripped to the waist, with their faces painted gaudy red, blue, and yellow raced up the gangplank. Some had braided their hair and others were decorated with beads and headdresses. But the people knew that real Indians they were not!

The shock of seeing them momentarily stilled the crowd. Then shouts erupted, as they watched the band of men start to clear the decks of their chests of tea right into Boston Harbor! She frantically scanned the faces of the "Indians." William, William where are you? Then, in her line of vision came an even

more startling sight: a tall broad shouldered Plimouth "Indian"
with piercing blue eyes, striding aboard the deck of the nearest
ship. He looked up, as if feeling a set of eyes upon him, and was
equally startled to see a pretty, red-haired girl almost hidden in a
voluminous blue cloak. He stared for a moment, then his right
eyelid dropped in a solemn wink, as he raised his hatchet.

Patience had seen enough. She used her elbows and the heels
of her boots to persuade those who did not want to move. A
strapping fellow fell back, growling at her shove, but laughed
good naturedly when he saw her size. "Come down to the docks,
Missy," he called to her back, "we can use you loadin' the ships."
She was beyond caring as she fought her way back through the
people, back to the roads leading away from the waterfront, and
up Salem Street to the Wentworth house. Lily was waiting
anxiously just inside the back door.

"I told them all you'd gone to bed." She drawled the last
word out as she pulled Patience inside. "It's been ever so noisy. I
was ever so worried. What is going on out there? Did you see
Thomas?"

"Yes," Patience responded hollowly, and with great
weariness, "I did."

# Chapter 12

Patience tossed and turned throughout the sleepless night. Drenched with perspiration, she lay under the quilt as images of tea hurling into the still, black, harbor waters flashed before her eyes. Even exhaustion did not allow her to escape into sleep. She could see the men wielding tomahawks, their bodies glistening with sweat, even in the frigid cold. They had ripped open the wooden chests and heaved the insides over the railings of the ships. In haste, some boxes had been thrown whole into the pool of darkness, crashing haphazardly into one another, until finally sinking from the weight of the water. She squeezed her eyes tightly shut, hoping to forget, but it did not help. The burly, scarred man jammed in next to her at the pier had screamed shrilly, "It's a party, a tea party!" But he was wrong. It had been no party! The stench from the stagnant harbor and the jeers of the people had been too intense, too frightening.

Her mind was filled with images of the "Mohawks," creeping along in a ragged pattern toward the wharf, while some from the Meeting House and the streets came running after them, pushing to be near. The devastation at the wharf had shocked her into reality. That, plus the recognition of Thomas' face under the war paint. She knew there must have been others in the "Indian" band that she would also have known had she looked more closely, but the faces had blurred together after she had seen him.

As she made her escape, the ragged old woman in her path gleefully chuckled, "Heard tell three hundred and forty-two crates is now food for them fishes." Fighting her way back through the men, women, and even children, who swarmed toward the ships, she had been elbowed and shoved as she forced her way against the human tide. Once free of them, she had raced the rest of the way as if chased by demons, stealthily entering the Wentworth house with Lily's help. Lily, who in spite of Henry's scolding, had stayed hidden in the kitchen for who knew how long. Her memory of changing, then slipping beneath the bed covers was hazier. Spent as she had been, she had lain restlessly awake, not able to bury in sleep what had happened.

Father preached that ruining another's property was a sin. What would her parents say if they knew what she had done? This time she could not pretend she had been just an innocent messenger. She had read the note before passing it, hastily resealed, to Master Wheeler. Its scribbled words had set out the plan for the waiting men to dress as Indians and dump the British tea into the harbor. This time, she had deliberately helped.

Almost sick with fear, she shook off the suffocating quilt and, wrapped in her bedtime shawl, rose to pace the dark silent room. How would the British retaliate? They had all committed treason against the government. Her role would likely remain hidden only because of the care that William and Master Wheeler had taken in protecting her identity. But suppose Thomas had been recognized, especially by someone who would identify him to British authorities. Then what would happen?

She cracked open one of the shutters and stared up at the bright moon while she forced herself to face what she had done. Was she honestly sorry for what had happened, or simply afraid that they all might be caught? She took refuge in the warmth of the shawl and searched for an answer. Minutes, seeming like hours, ticked by while she judged the deed without excuse. In the end she felt better. She knew in her heart there had been no real choice. The King and Parliament would not have paid attention to less. She closed the shutter against the moonlight and returned to bed. Now all that was left was fear of what England would do. Finally, just before dawn, exhaustion overtook her, letting her drift into a troubled sleep.

♦ ♦ ♦

Morning sounds brought Patience to a sleepy consciousness. The massive front door slammed constantly and male voices, overlaid with heavy footsteps, punctuated the air.

Her eyes barely open, she started to get up. Suddenly there was a quick push against the connecting door. Anne stood in the entrance, still in her flowing nightdress, and hanging onto the doorjamb for support. "Oh please, Patience, I'm so afraid!" Her cheeks were streaked with tears. "Do you know what happened last night?" She raced on without taking a breath. "Something horrible, something terrible! You won't believe it. I can't. The British tea was thrown into the harbor! Indians they say. How can that be?" She gulped back a sob. "Men have been coming since early morning to speak to Father. I can hear them from my room. They are all worried about what England will do. They say that the British soldiers at Castle William are ready to enter the city and that maybe more troops will come! They're sure the King won't stand for this insult." Her voice ended in a muffled cry.

Patience jumped up and helped her to the bed. Anne sat on the edge and put her head in her hands. Patience stared at her helplessly. Last night weighed heavily on them both. Patience started to put her arm around Anne's shoulder, but then stopped. What could she say? Anne, completely defeated, raised her head and gazed hopelessly at her best friend. The look cut Patience to the core and she tried to give Anne something to hold on to.

"Maybe they're wrong," she said, forcing an element of confidence into her voice. "Maybe nothing will happen. Pray God, because of this maybe England will even change its mind about the tea tax."

But even to her own ears the words sounded ridiculously foolish. Anne shook her head wearily, "I don't believe that. It wouldn't be possible." She sat up straight. "There's nothing for us to do here. I can't stand not knowing what's going on. Let's go downstairs." They dressed, and Patience helped Anne down to the dining room.

The room was in total disarray. The French crystal chandeliers and fragile English porcelain looked out of place. Coats and hats had been thrown without thought over chairs not otherwise taken by the men crushed together around the table. Henry had given up trying to maintain order and instead rushed about keeping mugs filled with hot cider and something stronger. Master Hancock, Boston's wealthiest merchant, sat with

Deirdre's father at one end of the room while at the other, William leaned close, intent upon hearing every word said. Anne's father who, had he noticed the girls, would not have allowed them to stay, paid no attention, so they sat together, white-faced, in chairs near the door. They listened with increasing alarm.

William raised his voice, "You know Ezra Broderick—a more dedicated Loyalist doesn't exist—well he has it on good authority that Hutchinson is furious over the incident and has already dispatched a strong message to King George!"

Master Foster interrupted, "Yes, yes, he is one of those who've already ordered their households to pack, so nervous are they about the violence of the situation, a 'near riot' they've called it!"

"That's not the way I heard it. No violence I heard," Master Wentworth said sharply, rising to walk the room. Patience silently agreed, although a small inner voice insistently reminded her how close it had been.

Master Hancock chimed in, "I heard the same reports, George. A show of solidarity was what it was. But, all the same, your move to Scituate couldn't be better timed. Boston is apt to be difficult for some time to come." There were barks of sarcastic laughter at his understatement.

"You're undoubtedly right. Best to have the women out of the city. I, of course, will remain here until matters are straightened out. It's only a matter of time before retaliation comes in some form. I hear those infernal Loyalists have already petitioned the Governor to allow them to move to Castle William for their safety." He clapped someone on the back at the far end of the table, a man with fierce eyes and a close-cropped head of hair. "England backed off with the sugar tax and the quartering of soldiers. They'll never do that again. We must be ready."

As the girls listened intently to the speculation about England's response, Anne became more upset with each dire prediction. Soon Patience took her hand and whispered, "Why don't we go outside? It couldn't possibly be colder there than it is here." They walked out. Only William glanced up.

No sooner had they reached the hall, than Anne's eyes began to tear again. "I'm so worried Oliver won't be able to come back. What if his family objects to me?" A note of panic crept into her voice. "Now that he's an Earl, he must sit in the House of Lords. Because he's been here in the colonies, they'll surely look to him for advice about this business."

Patience stared at her with dawning awareness. Too consumed by her own worries, she had not even thought about Oliver who, with his father's death, would indeed be a member of Parliament, helping King George make the very policies that the men now sitting at the Wentworth table feared. Anne was right! What irony. She tried desperately to mask her thoughts as she threw on her cloak. They trudged out the side door and into the garden. Bundled against the blistering wind, they sat on the hard marble seat.

At last Anne broke the silence, her voice bleak and toneless. "You'll be leaving tomorrow. Then I'll again have only Lily to talk to. As wonderful as she is, it will be different. You don't tell me just what I want to hear, but what I need to hear. How will I do without you?"

Patience tried desperately to think of something hopeful to say. "You know how much I'll miss you too. But with your cast off tomorrow, things will seem much better. I—I'm sure you'll be so involved in moving to North River that you'll not even realize I'm gone." Anne looked at her disbelievingly, but Patience hurried on, unable to stop herself. "I know, but we'll write often and—" She remembered, "Why it's only a month until Prudence's wedding when we'll see each other again. Then before we know it, the summer will be here and you'll be coming to the Plimouth shore for a good long visit. We'll walk the beach and swing on the porch as we always have . . ." Her voice trailed off. Could it ever be the same again? Even she didn't believe that anymore.

Anne took a deep breath to control her trembling and with great effort spoke of something else. "So much has happened that I keep forgetting you've not seen your family since last summer. Are you anxious to go home?"

Patience slumped against the stone backrest, trying to hide from the blowing December wind, and thought of Plimouth and her family. "More than I ever imagined, except for missing you, of course." She looked solemnly at Anne. "When I left last July, life in Plimouth seemed so dull. My sisters' chatter about those interminable wedding plans bored me silly. Now many things are different. I really look forward to seeing everyone, but especially Prudence and Charity." She sighed. "I fear that, in the past, I often acted like a spoiled child, refusing to pay attention to what was important to them. As a matter of fact, I'm even looking forward to seeing Prudence's wedding clothes." She added wryly, "Although I have not missed the sewing at all."

"And you are certainly no better at it than when you left Plimouth," Anne added with a flash of her former mischievousness. They exchanged smiles. Finally Anne said in a small desolate voice, "I miss you already."

"I know. I feel the same, but I keep telling myself that I will see you again only short weeks from now." She stood up, wrapping the blue cloak more tightly around her body. "And now I'd better go back to the house and finish packing. Your father told me that the carriage will leave tomorrow morning at ten. I'm sure that now, after everything that's happened, he will find it even more important to have me quickly away."

They left the garden, gray with winter hibernation, and went back into the crisis and barely controlled confusion. Patience looked quickly around to see if William was in sight, but he had gone.

Anne went with Patience to her room while she completed packing. They talked aimlessly, skirting the topic of the fast approaching departure. The day passed quickly. Deirdre, closely chaperoned by two burly footmen, stopped in for a few minutes to say good-bye to Patience. No one spoke of the night past. No one spoke of Oliver.

The next morning Patience looked for Lily. Missing her in the pantry, she climbed the narrow back stairs to the third floor servants' quarters and knocked on the maid's closed door. Lily inched the door open only wide enough not to be thought of as rude. "Oh Patience. It's just you. I just needed to get something. I'm coming to the pantry right quick and can see you there."

"It's no bother, Lily. I just wanted to make sure that I didn't miss you. I wanted to thank you for all your help while I was here."

She held out a square package, elaborately wrapped with crisp white paper and a pink ribbon. Lily stepped out into the hall and clapped her hands in delight. "Oh my, you're so kind to me, just like Anne." She took the present carefully and looked at it from every angle, murmuring, "I don't want to rip the paper." She paused, weighing whether the box should be saved, then decided she couldn't wait, and removed the wrapping, folding it to use at another time.

She opened the door wider to slip the paper safely inside and Patience peeked into the room. The sparse furnishings, a plain iron bed and a tiny wooden bureau, were typical of those in servants' rooms everywhere. But here and there were objects of comparative splendor, a gold velvet pillow, a small lace coverlet, a Chinese porcelain vase, undoubtedly all gifts from Anne. In the corner of the room she saw a worn ladies trunk, filled with clothes, one dress crushed on top of another in no particular order. Perhaps that was where Lily kept clothes that did not fit in the minute bureau.

Lily whooped with delight. "It's beautiful," she said, gazing at the small lace handkerchief nestled in the package. Although not extravagant, it was the latest European fashion and newly arrived at Master Foster's shop.

"Only for church," she said more to herself than to Patience.

As Lily tried to take her hand, Patience hugged her close, and then held her at arm's length, smiling at her familiar face. "I shall miss you, Lily. I have never met anyone like you. But I'm sure this time Anne will bring you to Plimouth in the summer. We'll see each other again very shortly."

A tear rolled down Lily's cheek and she seemed about to say something, then she changed her mind and, instead, wiped her eyes with the back of her hand. She took a deep breath and mumbled, "Cook'll miss me; I'd better go before I get my ears cuffed."

Recalling Cook's temper, Patience patted Lily's shoulder, and the girls left the hallway, Lily to scurry back to the kitchen and Patience to find Anne. Anne was still in her bedroom, sitting at the window, gazing thoughtfully outside. It had snowed lightly and, covered with pristine white, the dormant garden looked less bleak than the day before. Patience sat next to her on the window seat and began the comforting phrases she had rehearsed on her way to the room. "It's only a month until Prudence's wedding. When you come to Plimouth. We'll talk and talk." She stopped when she saw how calm and controlled Anne was.

"I shall miss you, Patience, more than I can say. It's been like having the sister I so often wanted." Anne threw her arms around her and held on as if she would never let go. Patience's eyes filled with tears. The girls sat silently several minutes until Mistress Wentworth knocked on the door to tell them the time to leave had come. They all walked downstairs, Patience helping Anne for the last time.

The carriage had been brought around and the horses, roused from their warm stalls and anxious to be away, pawed the ground impatiently. Master Wentworth joined them in the turnabout, the strain of the crisis showing on his face. He handed her into the coach. "We will miss you, Patience, but I'm relieved you'll be safely out of the city." Through the open carriage door they exchanged promises that, with the Plimouth wedding close at hand, they would see each other again soon. Anne clasped Patience's hands tightly, then let go. She appeared determined to shed no further tears. Master Wentworth shut the door and the Boston visit ended.

♦ ♦ ♦

Isaac cracked the whip and the journey home began. This time the jostling ride was familiar and Patience paid no attention as they turned south and retraced the path to her hometown. The tavern stop for a midday meal was not nearly as intriguing as the first time. She was so caught up in thinking about the ruin of the tea and what the British might do that the trip seemed over almost before it began.

They crossed the bridge over the Jones River in Kingston, and she knew that she was crossing back into a life to which she would never again completely belong. She had been so innocent in July, a schoolgirl dreaming of excitement. She now knew that the price of excitement was often pain and fear. The Boston crisis, she was sure, had just begun.

The carriage had no sooner started down the familiar street, now covered with snow, than Ben and Samuel bounded down the steps of the weather-beaten parsonage and raced each other to the coach, laughing and yelling as they escorted her home.

The rest of the family, having taken turns watching for her from the parlor window, waited anxiously at the bottom of the front steps. As Isaac pulled the horses to a stop, they crowded toward the carriage and Samuel flung open the door without even waiting for the driver to dismount. Father didn't even seem to notice. Hands reached toward her eagerly and she was enveloped. She was so glad to be home! Even Jeremiah was there, hovering at the edge of the family circle. He said he'd come by just to welcome her, but she noticed that his eyes never left Prudence.

They walked together into the warmth of the house. Soon Isaac was bundled off to a neighboring inn for the night and the family huddled happily around the dining table. Jenny served up mugs of hot mulled cider "to warm the tired bones of the traveler."

Extra candles of celebration had been lit and the flames cast a warm glow on all they touched. Patience ran her eyes over the cozy and familiar room, so unlike the grandeur of the Wentworths'. She looked at the loving faces surrounding her. She was completely content. Father invited them to bow their heads in thanksgiving to the Lord. As soon as he intoned the last "amen," he turned to her, seated next to him in the position of honor. He unexpectedly took her hand. "Patience, before you are besieged by other questions, there is something I must know. My dear, a rider came from Boston early this morning with shocking news of a 'tea party.' Can it be that British tea was really thrown in the harbor? Do you know anything of this?"

She looked around the table. No one spoke. Slowly, carefully, she outlined the story, giving only the facts that could be found out by anyone. She desperately hoped that her face would not give away more. When she finished there was silence. Father was the first to speak. "If it had not been the tea, it would have been something else over which we confronted them. These difficulties have been brewing for too long. The Crown cannot continue to ignore our voices in matters that affect us so deeply."

Everyone murmured in agreement as if they had always felt that way. Had they and she had just not known? That could be. She had been so oblivious before as to what they had believed that—but, no matter, that was not the case any more. She was just relieved that now they all felt the same.

They continued to talk well into the night, of city things and those closer to home, like Samuel's joining the town militia, and the wedding. Patience noticed that Prudence and Jeremiah sat close together, and when she rose to get the gifts she had brought, she saw that they were holding hands under the table. Jeremiah professed to be delighted at her choice of a book of inspirational sermons. Patience smiled wryly as she remembered buying it from Master Wheeler as an excuse during her first delivery to the stationer's. It seemed so long ago. Charity was as talkative as ever, but now she spoke only of Matthew and how hardworking and ambitious he was. Patience simply listened, finding the everyday conversation soothing. Finally, the candles burned to nothing and Jeremiah left reluctantly, telling everyone that he was rising early to work on a sermon now that he had a new book to inspire him. Mother shooed the family off to bed, saying there was plenty of time to talk at breakfast.

Patience was surprised how tired she still felt the next day, but Mother reminded her, "Changes are always wearing. In a few days you'll return to Plimouth in spirit as well as in body." Matthew's father rushed over early in the morning to tell them that some, sympathetic to the "Boston doings," had burst into a shop in Marshfield, seized the stock of tea, and burned it in protest over British taxation. Father bowed his head, "Praise God, help us. It has started."

Later in the afternoon, Mistress Dunham—"as able as I've been in years, my dear"—dropped by for a minute and spoke optimistically of a visit to Boston to see Mistress Canfield. She seemed completely unaware that the city might no longer be a safe place to travel. Patience decided that she would not be the one to tell her. The rest of the day passed swiftly.

Patience went to bed early. Stretching out comfortably on her familiar iron bed, she dropped off to sleep immediately, but woke to a frantic banging on the front door. Momentarily disoriented, she struggled to her feet while Prudence lit a candle from the dying embers in the tiny fireplace. It was very late. What could be the matter? Only bad news came at this hour. Hastily wrapping in woolen bed comforters, Prudence and Charity stumbled behind Patience down the stairs, following the glow from the quickly lit parlor candles. Father had already opened the front door and was practically carrying an exhausted Master Wentworth into the room. Patience's heart sank at the sight of him. Had something happened to Anne? Mother ran to the kitchen for the dandelion wine, kept especially for medical emergencies. Samuel and Ben frantically tried to start a fire from the almost dead embers in the main fireplace. Father clutched Master Wentworth's arm and led him to the wing chair closest to the weak flames that the boys were desperately fanning. "George, George, what has happened?"

"It's Anne." A sob escaped from his rigid lips. "She has run off." There was a stunned silence. His words were completely unexpected. Run off? What was he talking about?

Master Wentworth poured out those words he had memorized on his ride from Boston. "There was a note this morning—I think it was only this morning. She had it delivered to us as soon as she and Lily set sail. She has gone to be with that blasted Englishman!" He slumped in the chair, his eyes strained and dull. He stared mutely at Father while he gathered strength to begin again. They waited silently in the damp, dark, room barely warmed by the pitiful fire. "Anne wrote she feared the tea incident would result in such retaliation that that man could never return." He could not even bring himself to speak Oliver's name. "My daughter is on the high seas, headed for a country where she has no family and no resources! Pray God, she is only a child!" His voice broke again.

Mother knelt beside him and placed a large goblet of wine in his hand, then held it for him, waiting until he gulped it gratefully. The drink seemed to steady him a bit and, within minutes, traces of color returned to his face. He continued falteringly. "My wife has taken sick. I'm not sure if she'll ever be the same. When we read the note, I rushed to the harbor to try to have the ship stopped, but it had already departed to the open seas. They say no ships will sail until further notice."

Patience could not believe his words. He must be wrong. But even as that thought surfaced, she remembered what she had seen on her last morning in Boston, and much of it began to make awful sense. The image of Lily's trunk packed with clothes and Anne's clinging farewell rushed to mind. Hearing Master Wentworth speak her name, she looked at the poor man who remained crumpled in the chair.

"Patience tried to warn us, but we brushed her words aside, so sure the infatuation was waning. How could we have been so wrong?"

"George," Father bent over and put his arm around Master Wentworth's shoulder. "You and Margaret must not blame yourselves," he consoled. "We act as we think best for our children."

The warmth of Father's arm seemed to quiet him. He sipped again from the goblet and then pulled a letter from his pocket. "Patience, Anne left this envelope addressed to you. I wanted to bring it here directly, and see if you could tell me anything else."

With trembling hands, she unsealed the note and read it aloud.

*"Dearest Patience,*

*"I am sorry I could not tell you of my plans. I was afraid you would try to change my mind. You may be right that England will not force the tea tax, but I could not chance that I would never see my dear Oliver again.*

*"I will truly miss my parents. I know that my actions will cause them much grief and ask you to console them as best you can.*

*"I long to see you again, and I'm sure that I shall. Until then, I shall wear your pin always to remember our friendship. I am sending the painting for you to hold until we see each other again.*

*"Your loving friend, Anne."*

The tiny painting fell into Patience's hand, a picture of two lifelong friends, carefree and happy.

# Epilogue

Patience stood with her back to the pulpit and surveyed the inside of the pristine church. The silence and simplicity brought a welcome sense of peace. The sun shone through the spotless windows onto the polished wooden pews, pouring its light into the crevices worn by generations of worshipers. Entrusted with the task of making sure that the small church reflected its pride in Prudence's wedding, she had worked diligently for two days, scrubbing and waxing to perfection. The solitary labor had given her the time she needed to think about all that had happened. Now with the ceremony only a little more than an hour away, she had dressed in her wedding best, the very dress that had made its debut at the Governor's mansion, and had come to take a last look. She walked down the aisle of the church in which she had spent her entire life and slipped into a back pew. Her thoughts returned to the past few weeks.

Master Wentworth had been sick with grief. She had understood not only the reasons he gave, but the ones he did not, and had tried to reassure him that Oliver had not persuaded Anne to leave, as he believed. Fortunately, Anne had shared with her the one and only letter Oliver had sent from England. He had talked of their great love and of returning soon to claim her as his wife. Patience had not said anything about Master Wentworth's fear that the escalating trouble between England and the colonies would mean a permanent break with Anne, because she was afraid he was right. Father had also tried to reassure the stricken man. "I'm sure that Patience is correct about the young man's character. You must have faith that you have taught Anne well. We will pray for them both." Despite their pleas for him to rest,

Master Wentworth had left immediately for the lonely ride back to Boston.

Afterward Patience and her parents had continued to talk long into the night, instinctively glad that they had each other. Patience had known then that eventually, when the time was right, she would tell them what she had done. At that moment she had felt sure that they would understand.

She shifted on the hard bench, trying to make herself more comfortable, and her thoughts drifted toward William Allen and how their friendship had been interrupted. She looked out the nearest window and thought about what might have been. She smiled to herself. He was impressive and definitely interested in her, but still . . .

She finally allowed herself to think about the subject she knew she had been avoiding: Thomas. The Warrens had come by specifically to ask her about Boston and about their son. They had been happy when she told them all she could of his job, and the Dudleys, and how he looked and how well he was. She knew he was due back in Plimouth because they had said as much. She wondered if he would call on her and, if so, for what reason. Had her warm friendship with him become something more? She felt so, but was afraid he might not agree. She had come to realize that caring for someone was much more complicated than she had thought it would be. She knew now that she had been more worried about Thomas' part in the "tea party" than she had been about her own difficult journey out that evening. How had he felt when he saw her?

A small noise let her know that she was not the only one in the church. She turned, thinking to greet an early guest, and saw Thomas in the vestibule, looking at her through the open doors. He walked deliberately over to the pew, slid in beside her, and took her hand in both of his.

"Well, and who have we here?" he said teasingly. "The daring Miss Burgess, I believe."

Patience looked up at him with some indignation, trying to pull her hand out of his grasp. His hold tightened.

"Daring indeed," she replied smartly. "And who was it parading on the deck of that ship for everyone to see, I wonder."

"Yes, but I knew what I was doing!" Patience detected a superior tone.

"Are you implying I was doing anything?" she countered sharply. "And even if I had been," she hurried on, "I'd have been well aware of the risks."

"So I was told." He shook his head ruefully. "It was the only thing that kept me from taking *Schoolmaster* William Allen apart piece by piece when I learned what you had done." He finished forcefully, "He and I did not separate on the best of terms."

"How did you find out about me?"

"I wanted to know just what you and he were doing on your walks, so I asked him. He didn't wish to tell me until I . . ." he paused to seek the right word, "persuaded him it would be for the best."

"Well, I never—" she began with some exasperation.

"That is right. You will never. Never be involved in something again that can put you in such danger." He sighed heavily. "It's a good thing I like spirited women."

Patience stood up and looked him in the eye, so there could be no misunderstanding. "How I follow my beliefs is my own choice. I, for my part, do not like bossy would-be lawyers who think they can make decisions for me."

Thomas rose slowly from his seat and, reaching over, put a strong arm around her waist, pulling her close. His eyes looked right into hers. "You will," he whispered. "You will learn to, and lead me a merry chase in the process. I can see that." He bent toward her. Her lips closed the distance to his.

## Historical Note

Between March and May, 1774 the English Parliament passed the Coercive Acts on all the American colonies. The Acts included specific retaliation on the city of Boston: the port of Boston was ordered closed until the cost of the tea was reimbursed.

England did not know that by exacting such punishment there would be a revolutionary reaction.

And, as they say, the rest is history . . .